Enid Blyton

The
Adventures
of the
Wishing-
Chair

EGMONT

EGMONT

First published in Great Britain in 1937 by Newnes
This edition published 2014 by Egmont UK Limited
The Yellow Building, 1 Nicholas Road
London, W11 4AN

Enid Blyton ®
Enid Blyton's signature is a Registered Trademark of Hodder
and Stoughton Limited
Text copyright © Hodder and Stoughton Limited
Illustrations copyright © Hodder and Stoughton Limited

ISBN 978 1 4052 9016 6

www.egmont.co.uk

A CIP catalogue record for this title is available from the British Library

Printed and bound in Great Britain by the CPI Group

4043/52

CONTENTS

CHAPTER 1

THE STRANGE OLD SHOP

The adventures really began on the day that Mollie and Peter went out to spend thirty-five pence on a present for their mother's birthday.

They emptied the money out of their money-box and counted it.

'Thirty-five!' said Peter. 'Good! Now, what shall we buy Mother?'

'Mother loves old things,' said Mollie. 'If we could find an old shop somewhere, full of old things – you know, funny spoons, quaint vases, old glasses and beads – something of that sort would be lovely for Mother. She would love an old tea-caddy to keep the tea in, I'm sure, or perhaps an old, old vase.'

'All right,' said Peter. 'We'll go and find one of those shops this very day. Put on your hat and come on, Mollie.'

Off they went, and ran into the town.

'It's a shop with the word "Antiques" over it that we want,' said Peter. 'Antiques means old things. Just look out for that, Mollie.'

But there seemed to be no shop with the word 'Antiques' printed over it at all. The children left the main street and went down a little turning. There were more shops there, but still not the one they wanted. So on they went and came to a small, narrow street whose houses were so close that there was hardly any light in the road!

And there, tucked away in the middle, was the shop with 'Antiques' printed on a label inside the dirty window.

'Good!' said Peter. 'Here is a shop that sells old things. Look, Mollie, do you see that strange little vase with swans set all round it? I'm sure Mother would like that. It is marked twenty-five pence. We could buy that *and* some flowers to put in it!'

So into the old dark shop they went. It was so dark that the children stumbled over some piled-up rugs on the floor. Nobody seemed to be about. Peter went to the counter and rapped on it. A tiny door at the back opened and out came the strangest little man, no higher than the countertop. He had pointed ears like a pixie. The children stared at him in surprise. He looked very cross, and spoke sharply.

'What do you want, making a noise like that?'

'We want to buy the vase with swans round it,' said Peter.

Muttering and grumbling to himself, the little chap picked up the vase and pushed it across the counter. Peter put down the money. 'Can I have some paper to wrap the vase in?' he asked politely. 'You see, it's for my mother's birthday, and I don't want her to see me carrying it home.'

Grumbling away to himself, the little man went to a pile of boxes at the back of the shop and began to open one to look for a piece of paper. The children watched. To their enormous surprise a large black cat with golden eyes

jumped out of the box and began to spit and snarl at the little man. He smacked it and put it back again. He opened another box.

Out of that came a great wreath of green smoke that wound about the shop and smelt strange. The little man caught hold of it as if it were a ribbon and tried to stuff it back into the box again. But it broke off and went wandering away. How he stamped and raged! The children felt quite frightened.

'We'd better go without the paper,' whispered Mollie to Peter, but just then another extraordinary thing happened. Out of the next box came a crowd of blue butterflies. They flew into the air, and the little man shouted with rage again. He darted to the door and shut it, afraid that the butterflies would escape. To the children's horror they saw him lock the door too and put the key into his pocket!

'We can't get out till he lets us go!' said Mollie. 'Oh dear, why did we ever come here? I'm sure that little man is a gnome or something.'

The little fellow opened another box, and, hey presto! out jumped a red fox! It gave a short bark and then began to run about the shop, its nose to the ground. The children were half afraid of being bitten, and they both sat in an old chair together, their legs drawn up off the ground, out of the way of the fox.

It was the most curious shop they had ever been in! Fancy keeping all those queer things in boxes! Really, there must be magic about somewhere. It couldn't be a proper shop.

The children noticed a little stairway leading off the shop about the middle, and suddenly at the top of this, there appeared somebody else! It was somebody tall and thin, with such a long beard that it swept the ground. On his head was a pointed hat that made him seem taller still.

'Look!' said Mollie. 'Doesn't he look like a wizard?'

'Tippit, Tippit, what are you doing?' cried the newcomer, in a strange, deep voice, like the rumbling of faraway thunder.

'Looking for a piece of paper!' answered the little man, in a surly tone. 'And all I can find is butterflies and foxes, a black cat, and –'

'What! You've dared to open those boxes!' shouted the other angrily. He stamped down the stairs, and then saw the children.

'And who are *you*?' he asked, staring at them. 'How dare you come here?'

'We wanted to buy this vase,' said Peter, frightened.

'Well, seeing you are here, you can help Tippit to catch the fox,' said the tall man, twisting his beard up into a knot and tying it under his chin. 'Come on!'

'I don't want to,' said Mollie. 'He might bite me. Unlock the door and let us go out.'

'Not till the fox and all the butterflies are caught and put into their boxes again,' said the tall man.

'Oh dear!' said Peter, making no movement to get out of the chair, in which he and Mollie were still sitting with their legs drawn up. 'I do wish we were safely at home!'

And then the most extraordinary thing of all happened! The chair they were in began to creak and groan, and suddenly it rose up in the air, with the two children in it! They held tight, wondering whatever was happening! It flew to the door, but that was shut. It flew to the window, but that was shut too.

Meantime the wizard and Tippit were running after it, crying out in rage. 'How dare you use our wishing-chair! Wish it back, wish it back!'

'I shan't!' cried Peter. 'Go on, wishing-chair, take us home!'

The chair finding that it could not get out of the door or the window, flew up the little stairway. It nearly got stuck in the doorway at the top, which was rather narrow, but just managed to squeeze itself through. Before the children could see what the room upstairs was like, the chair flew to the window there, which was open, and out it went into the street. It immediately rose up very high indeed, far beyond the housetops, and flew towards the children's home. How amazed they were! And how tightly they clung to the arms! It would be dreadful to fall!

'I say, Mollie, can you hear a flapping noise?' said Peter. 'Has the chair got wings anywhere?'

Mollie peeped cautiously over the edge of the chair. 'Yes!' she said. 'It has a little red wing growing out of each leg, and they make the flapping noise! How queer!'

The chair began to fly downwards. The children saw that they were just over their garden.

'Go to our playroom, Chair,' said Peter quickly. The chair went to a big shed at the bottom of the garden. Inside was a playroom for the children, and here they kept all their toys and books, and could play any game they liked. The chair flew in at the open door and came to rest on the floor. The children jumped off and looked at one another.

'The first real adventure we've ever had in our lives!' said Mollie, in delight. 'Oh, Peter, to think we've got a magic chair – a wishing-chair!'

'Well, it isn't really ours,' said Peter, putting the swan vase carefully down on the table. 'Perhaps we had better send it back to that shop.'

'I suppose we had,' said Mollie sadly. 'It would be so lovely if we could keep it!'

'Go back to your shop, Chair,' commanded Peter. The chair didn't move an inch! Peter spoke to it again; still the chair wouldn't move! There it was and there it stayed. And suddenly the children noticed that its little red wings had gone from the legs! It looked just an ordinary chair now!

'See, Mollie! The chair hasn't any wings!' cried Peter. 'It can't fly. I expect it is only when it grows wings that it can fly. It must just have grown them when we were sitting in it in the shop. What luck for us!'

'Peter! Let's wait till the chair has grown wings again, and then get in it and see where it goes!' said Mollie, her face red with excitement. 'Oh, do let's!'

'Well, it might take us anywhere!' said Peter doubtfully. 'Still, we've always wanted adventures, Mollie, haven't we? So we'll try! The very next time our wishing-chair grows wings, we'll sit in it and fly off again!'

'Hurrah!' said Mollie. 'I hope it will be tomorrow!'

CHAPTER 2
THE GIANT'S CASTLE

Each day Mollie and Peter ran down to their playroom in the garden, and looked at their wishing-chair to see if it had grown wings again. But each time they were disappointed. It hadn't.

'It may grow them in the night,' said Peter. 'But we can't possibly keep coming here in the dark to see. We must just be patient.'

Sometimes the children sat in the chair and wished themselves away, but nothing happened at all. It was really very disappointing.

And then one day the chair grew its wings again. It was a Saturday afternoon too, which was very jolly, as the children were not at school. They ran down to the playroom and opened the door, and the very first thing they saw was that the chair had grown wings! They couldn't help seeing this, because the chair was flapping its wings about as if it was going to fly off!

'Quick! Quick!' shouted Peter, dragging Mollie to the chair. 'Jump in. It's going to fly!'

They were just in time! The chair rose up in the air, flapping its wings strongly, and made for the door. Out it went and rose high into the air at once. The children clung on tightly in the greatest delight.

'Where do you suppose it is going?' asked Peter.

'Goodness knows!' said Mollie. 'Let it take us wherever it wants to! It will be exciting, anyhow. If it goes back to that funny shop, we can easily jump off and run away when it goes in at the door.'

But the chair didn't go to the old shop. Instead it kept on steadily towards the west, where the sun was beginning to sink. By and by a high mountain rose up below, and the children looked down at it in astonishment. On the top was an enormous castle.

'Where's this, I wonder?' said Peter. 'Oh, I say, Mollie, the chair is going down to the castle!'

Down it went, flapping its rose-red wings. Soon it came to the castle roof, and instead of going lower and finding a door or a window, the chair found a nice flat piece of roof and settled down there with a sigh, as if it were quite tired out!

'Come on, Mollie! Let's explore!' said Peter excitedly. He jumped off the chair and ran to a flight of enormous steps that led down to the inside of the castle. He peeped down. No one was about.

'This is the biggest castle I ever saw,' said Peter. 'I wonder who lives here. Let's go and see!'

They went down the steps, and came to a big staircase leading from a landing. On every side were massive doors, bolted on the outside.

'I hope there are no prisoners inside!' said Mollie, half afraid.

The stairs suddenly ended in a great hall. The

children stood and looked in astonishment. Sitting at
an enormous table was a giant as big as six men. His
eyes were on a book, and he was trying to add up figures.

'Three times seven, three times seven, three times
seven!' he muttered to himself. 'I never can remember.
Where's that miserable little pixie? If he doesn't know, I'll
turn him into a black beetle!'

The giant lifted up his head and shouted so loudly
that both children put their hands over their ears. 'Binky!
Binky!'

A pixie, not quite so big as the children, came running
out of what looked like a scullery. He held an enormous
boot in one hand, and a very small boot-brush in the other.

'Stop cleaning my boots and listen to me!' ordered the

giant. 'I can't do my sums again. I'm adding up all I spent last week and it won't come right. What are three times seven?'

'Three times seven?' said the pixie, with a frightened look on his little pointed face.

'That's what I said,' thundered the bad-tempered giant.

'I know they are the same as seven times three,' said the pixie.

'Well, I don't know what seven times three are either!' roared the giant. '*You* tell me! What's the good of having a servant who doesn't know his tables? Quick – what are three times seven?'

'I d-d-d-don't know!' stammered the poor pixie.

'Then I'll lock you into the top room of the castle till you *do* know!' cried the giant, in a rage. He picked up the pixie and went to the stairs. Then he saw the children standing there, and he stopped in astonishment.

'Who are you, and what are you doing here?' he asked.

'We've just come on a flying visit,' said Peter boldly. '*We* know what three times seven are – and seven times three too. So, if you let that pixie go, we'll tell you.'

'You tell me, then, you clever children!' cried the giant, delighted.

'They are twenty-one,' said Peter.

The giant, still holding the pixie tightly in his hand, went across to the table and added up some figures.

'Yes – twenty-one,' he said. 'Now why didn't I think of that? Good!'

'Let the pixie go,' begged Mollie.

'Oh no!' said the giant, with a wicked grin. 'He shall be

shut up in the top room of my castle, and *you* shall be my servants instead, and help me to add up my sums! Come along with me whilst I shut up Binky.'

He pushed the two angry children in front of him and made them go all the way up the stairs until they came to the topmost door. The giant unbolted it and pushed the weeping pixie inside. Then he bolted it again and locked it.

'Quick!' whispered Peter to Mollie. 'Let's race up these steps to the roof and get on to our magic chair.'

So, whilst the giant was locking the door, the two of them shot up the steps to the roof. The giant didn't try to stop them. He stood and roared with laughter.

'Well, I don't know how you expect to escape *that* way!' he said. 'You'll have to come down the steps again, and I shall be waiting here to catch you. Then what a spanking you'll get!'

The children climbed out on to the flat piece of castle roof. There was their chair, standing just where they had left it, its red wings gleaming in the sun. They threw themselves into it, and Peter cried, 'Go to the room where that little pixie Binky is!'

The chair rose into the air, flew over the castle roof, and then down to a big window. It was open, and the chair squeezed itself inside. Binky the pixie was there, sitting on the floor, weeping. When he saw the chair coming in, with the two children sitting in it, he was so astonished that he couldn't even get up off the floor!

'Quick!' cried Mollie. 'Come into this chair, Binky. We'll help you to escape!'

'Who's talking in there?' boomed the giant's enormous voice, and the children heard the bolts being undone and the key turned to unlock the door!

'Quick, quick, Binky!' shouted Peter, and he dragged the amazed pixie to the magic chair. They all three sat in it, huddled together, and Peter shouted, 'Take us home!'

The door flew open and the giant rushed in just as the chair sailed out of the window. He ran to the window and made a grab at the chair. His big hand knocked against a leg, and the chair shook violently. Binky nearly fell off, but Peter grabbed him and pulled him back safely. Then they sailed high up into the air, far out of reach of the angry giant!

'We've escaped!' shouted Peter. 'What an adventure!

Cheer up, Binky! We'll take you home with us! You shall live with us, if you like. We have a fine playroom at the end of our garden. You can live there and no one will know. What fun we'll have with you and the wishing-chair!'

'You are very kind to me,' said Binky gratefully. 'I shall love to live with you. I can take you on many, many adventures!'

'Hurrah!' shouted the two children. 'Look, Binky, we're going down to our garden.'

Soon they were safely in the garden, and the chair flew in at the open door of the playroom. Its wings disappeared, and it settled itself down with a long sigh, as if to say, 'Home again!'

'You can make a nice bed of the cushions from the sofa,' said Mollie to the pixie. 'And I'll give you a rug from the hall chest to cover yourself with. We must go now, because it is past our tea-time. We'll come and see you again tomorrow. Good luck!'

CHAPTER 3
THE GRABBIT GNOMES

It was such fun to have a real live pixie to play with! Mollie and Peter went to their playroom every day and talked with Binky, whom they had so cleverly rescued from the giant's castle. He refused to have anything to eat, because he said he knew the fairies in the garden, and they would bring him anything he needed.

'Binky, will you do something for us?' asked Mollie. 'You know we can't be with the magic chair always to watch when it grows wings, but if you could watch it for us, and come and tell us when you see it has wings, then we could rush to our playroom and go on another adventure. It would be lovely if you'd do that.'

'Of course,' said Binky, who was a most obliging, merry little fellow. 'I'll never take my eyes off the chair!'

Well, will you believe it, that very night, just as Binky was going off to sleep, and the playroom was in darkness, he felt a strange little wind blowing from somewhere; it was the chair waving its wings about! Binky was up in a trice, and ran out of the playroom to the house. He knew which the children's room was, and he climbed up the old pear tree and knocked on the window.

It wasn't long before Mollie and Peter, each in warm

dressing-gowns, were running down to the playroom. They lighted a candle and saw the chair's red wings once more.

'Come on!' cried Peter, jumping into the chair. 'Where are we off to this time, I wonder?'

Mollie jumped in too, and Binky squeezed himself beside them. The chair was indeed very full.

It flew out of the door and up into the air. The moon was up, and the world seemed almost as light as day. The chair flew to the south, and then went downwards into a strange little wood that shone blue and green.

'Hallo, hallo! We're going to visit the Grabbit Gnomes,' said the pixie. 'I don't like that! They grab everything they can, especially things that don't belong to them! We must be careful they don't grab our wishing-chair!'

The chair came to rest in a small clearing, near to some queer toadstool houses. The doors were in the great thick stalks, and the windows were in the top part. No one was about.

'Oh, do let's explore this strange village!' cried Mollie, in delight. 'I do want to!'

'Well, hurry up, then,' said Binky nervously. 'If the Grabbit Gnomes see us here, they will soon be trying to grab this, that and the other.'

The two children ran off to the toadstool houses and looked at them. They really were lovely. How Mollie wished she had one at home in the garden! It would be so lovely to have one to live in.

'Whatever is Binky doing?' said Peter, turning round to look.

'He's got a rope or something,' said Mollie, in surprise. 'Oh, don't let's bother about him, Peter. Do look here! There are six little toadstools all laid ready for breakfast! Fancy! They use them for tables as well as for houses!'

Suddenly there was a loud shout from a nearby toadstool house.

'Robbers! Burglars!'

Someone was leaning out of the window of a big toadstool house, pointing to the children. In a trice all the Grabbit Gnomes woke up, and came pouring out of their houses. 'Robbers! What are you doing here? Robbers!'

'No, they're not,' said Binky, pushing his way through the crowd of excited gnomes. 'They are only children adventuring here.'

'How did you come?' asked a gnome at once.

'We came in our wishing-chair,' said Mollie, and then she wished she hadn't answered. For the Grabbit Gnomes

17

gave a yell of delight and rushed off to where their chair was standing in the moonlight.

'We've always wanted one, we've always wanted one!' they shouted. 'Come on! Let's take it safely to our cave where we hide our treasures!'

'But it's ours!' cried Peter indignantly. 'Besides, how shall we get back home if you take our chair?'

But the gnomes didn't pay any attention to him. They raced off to the chair, and soon there wasn't a tiny piece of the chair to be seen, for, to Peter's dismay, all the little gnomes piled themselves into it, and sat there – on the seat, the back, the arms, everywhere!

'Go to our treasure-cave!' they shouted. The chair flapped its red wings and rose up. The gnomes gave a yell of triumphant delight:

'We're off! Goodbye!'

'Oooh! Look!' said Mollie suddenly. 'There's something hanging down from the chair. What is it?'

'It's a rope!' said Peter. 'Oh, Binky, you clever old thing! You've tied it to the leg of the chair, and the other end is tied to that tree trunk over there. The chair can't fly away!'

'No,' said Binky, with a grin. 'It can't! I know those Grabbit Gnomes! I may not know what three times seven are, but I *do* know what robbers these gnomes are! Well, they won't find it easy to get away!'

The chair rose up high until the rope was so tightly stretched that it could go no farther. Then the chair came to a stop. There it hovered in the air, flapping its wings, but not moving one scrap. The gnomes shouted at it and yelled, but it was no good. It couldn't go any farther.

'Well, the gnomes are safe for a bit,' said Binky, grinning. 'Now what about exploring this village properly, children?'

So the two spent half an hour peeping into the quaint toadstool houses; and Binky gave them gnome-cake and gnome-lemonade, which were perfectly delicious.

All this time the gnomes were sitting up in the wishing-chair, high above the trees, shaking their fists at the children, and yelling all kinds of threats. They were certainly well caught, for they could go neither up nor down.

'Now, we'd better go home,' said Binky suddenly, pointing to the east. 'Look! – it will soon be dawn. Now listen to me. I am going to pull that chair down to earth again with your help. We will pull it down quickly, and it will land on the ground with such a bump that all the gnomes will be thrown off. Whilst they are picking themselves up, we will jump into the chair, and off we'll go.'

'Good idea!' grinned Peter. So he and Mollie and Binky went to the rope and pulled hard, hand over hand. The chair came down from the air rapidly, and when it reached the ground it gave such a bump that every single gnome was thrown off.

'Oooooh!' they cried. 'You wait, you wicked children!'

But they *didn't* wait. Instead, the three of them jumped into the chair, and Peter called out, 'Take us home, please!'

Before the Grabbit Gnomes could take hold of the chair, it had risen up into the air. But the gnomes pulled at the rope, and down came the chair again.

'Quick! Cut the rope!' shouted Peter to Binky. Poor Binky! He was feeling in every one of his many pockets for his knife, and he couldn't find it. The gnomes pulled hard at the rope, and the chair went down still farther.

And then Binky found the knife! He leaned over the chair-arm, slashed at the rope and cut it. At once the chair bounded up into the air, free!

'Home, home!' sang Peter, delighted. 'I say! Talk about adventures! Every one seems more exciting then the last! Wherever shall we go next?'

CHAPTER 4
THE HO-HO WIZARD

One day when Peter and Mollie ran down to see Binky the pixie in their playroom, they found him reading a letter and groaning loudly.

'What's the matter, Binky?' said the children, in surprise.

'Oh, I've had a letter from my cousin, Gobo,' said Binky. 'Gobo says that my village is very unhappy because a wizard has come to live there, called Ho-Ho. He is a horrid fellow, and walks about saying, "Ho, ho!" all the time, catching the little pixies to help him in his magic, and putting all kinds of spells on anyone that goes against him. I feel very unhappy.'

'Oh, Binky, we're so sorry!' said the children at once. 'Can't we help?'

'I don't think so,' said Binky sadly. 'But I would very much like to go off in the wishing-chair to my village, next time it grows wings, if you don't mind.'

'Of course!' said the children. Then Mollie cried out in delight, and pointed to the magic chair. 'Look! It's growing wings now! How lovely! It must have heard what we said.'

'We'll all go,' said Peter, feeling excited to think that yet another adventure had begun.

'Oh, no,' said Binky at once. 'I'd better go alone. This

wizard is a horrid one. He might quite well catch you, as you are clever children, and then think how dreadful I would feel!'

'I don't care!' said Peter. 'We're coming!'

He and Mollie went to the chair and sat firmly down in it. Binky went to it and sat down too, squeezing in between the two. 'You are such nice children!' he said happily.

The chair creaked, and before it could fly off, the pixie cried out loudly, 'Go to the village of Apple-pie!'

It flew slowly out of the door, flapping its rose-red wings. The children were used to flying off in the magic chair now, but they were just as excited as ever. The village of Apple-pie! How magic it sounded!

It didn't take them very long to get there. The chair put them down in the middle of the village street, and was at once surrounded by an excited crowd of pixies, who shook hands with Binky and asked him a hundred questions.

He talked at the top of his voice, explained who the children were, and why he had come. Then suddenly there was a great silence, and everyone turned pale. The Ho-ho Wizard was coming down the street!

He was a little fellow, with a long flowing cloak that swirled out as he walked and showed its bright golden lining. On his head he wore a round tight cap set with silver bells that tinkled loudly. He wore three pairs of glasses on his long nose, and a beard that hung in three pieces down to his waist. He really was a queer-looking fellow.

'Ho, ho!' he said, as he came near the pixies. 'What have we here? Visitors? And, bless us all, this is a wishing-chair, as sure as dogs have tails! Well, well, well!'

Nobody said anything at all. The wizard prodded the chair with a long stick and then turned to the children.

'Ho, ho!' he said, blinking at them through his pairs of glasses. 'Ho, ho! So you have a magic chair. Pray come to have a cup of cocoa with me this morning, and I will buy your chair from you.'

'But we don't want to sell it,' began Peter at once. The wizard turned round on him, and from his eyes there came what looked like real sparks. He was very angry.

'How dare you refuse me anything!' he cried. 'I will turn you into a –'

'We will come in half an hour,' stammered Binky, pushing Peter behind him. 'This boy did not understand how important you are, Sir Wizard.'

'Brrrrrrrrr!' said the wizard, and stalked off, his cloak flying out behind him.

'*Now* what are we to do?' said Peter, in dismay. 'Can't we get into the chair and fly off, Binky. Do let's!'

'No, no, don't!' cried all the pixies at once. 'If you do, Ho-ho will punish the whole village, and that will be terrible. Stay here and help us.'

'Come to my cousin Gobo's cottage and let us think,' said Binky. So the two children went with him and Gobo, who was really very like Binky, to a little crooked cottage at the end of the village. It was beautifully clean and neat, and the children sat down to eat coconut cakes and drink lemonade. Everyone was rather quiet. Then Peter's eyes began to twinkle, and he leaned over to Gobo.

'I say, Gobo, have you by any chance got a spell to put people to sleep?' he asked.

'Of course!' said Gobo, puzzled. 'Why?'

'Well, I have a fine plan,' said Peter. 'What about putting old Ho-ho to sleep?'

'What's the use of that?' said Binky and Gobo.

'Well – when he's asleep, we'll pop him into the magic chair, take him off somewhere and leave him, and then go back home ourselves!' said Peter. 'That would get rid of him for you, wouldn't it?'

'My goodness! That's an idea!' cried Binky, jumping up from his seat in excitement. 'Gobo! If only we could do it! Listen! Where's the sleepy-spell?'

'Here,' said Gobo, opening a drawer and taking out a tiny yellow thing like a mustard seed.

'Well, Peter has a bag of chocolates,' said Binky, 'and

he could put the sleepy spell into one of them and give it to Ho-ho.'

'But how do we know he'd take the right chocolate?' asked Mollie.

'We'll empty out all of them except one,' answered Binky, 'and that one Peter shall carry in the bag in his hand, and he must carry it as though it was something very precious indeed, and Ho-ho is sure to ask him what it is, and if Peter says it is a very special chocolate that he is not going to part with, or something like that, the old wizard is sure to be greedy enough to take it from him and eat it. Then he will fall asleep, and we'll take him off in the chair to old Dame Tap-Tap, who will be *so* pleased to have him! He once tried to turn her into a ladybird, so I don't think she will let him go in a hurry!'

'Good idea!' cried everyone, and Gobo danced round the room so excitedly that he fell over the coal scuttle and sent the fire-irons clanking to the floor. That made them all laugh, and they felt so excited that they could hardly empty out Peter's bag of chocolates on the table and choose one for the sleepy spell.

They chose a chocolate with a violet on top because it looked so grand. Peter made a little hole in it and popped in the spell. Then he left the rest of the chocolates with Gobo, who said he would enjoy them very much, put the violet one into the bag, and went off to get the wishing-chair with the others.

It was still standing in the marketplace, its red wings hanging down, for it was tired. Binky and Peter thought they might as well carry it to Ho-ho's cottage, which was only in the next street; so off they went, taking it on their shoulders.

Ho-ho was waiting for them, his wily face watching from a window. He opened the door, and they all went in with the chair.

'I see you have brought me the chair,' said Ho-ho. 'Very sensible of you! Now sit down and have a cup of cocoa.'

He poured out some very thin cocoa for them, made without any milk, and looked at them all sharply. He at once saw that Peter was holding something very carefully in his hand, which he did not even put down when he was drinking his cocoa.

'What have you got in your hand?' he asked.

'Something I want to keep!' said Peter at once.

'Show me,' said the wizard eagerly.

'No,' said Peter.

'SHOW ME!' ordered the wizard angrily.

Peter pretended to be frightened, and at once put the

paper bag on the table. The wizard took it and opened it. He took out the chocolate.

'Ho, ho! The finest chocolate I ever saw!' he said, and licked it to see what it tasted like.

'Don't eat it, oh, don't eat it!' cried Peter at once, pretending to be most upset. 'It's mine!'

'Well, now it's *mine*!' said the wizard, and he popped it into his mouth and chewed it up. And no sooner had he swallowed it than his head began to nod, his eyes closed, and he snored like twenty pigs grunting!

'The spell has worked, the spell has worked!' cried Peter, jumping about in excitement.

'Now, Peter, there's no time to jump and yell,' said Binky hurriedly. 'The spell may stop at any time, and we don't want to wake up the wizard till we've got him to Dame Tap-Tap's. Help me to put him into the chair.'

Between them they dumped the sleeping wizard into the chair. Then Mollie sat on one arm, Peter sat on the other, and Binky sat right on the top of the back. 'To Dame Tap-Tap!' he cried. At once the wishing-chair flapped its idle wings, flew out of the door, and up into the air, cheered by all the pixies in the village. What a thrill that was!

In about five minutes the chair flew downwards again to a small cottage set right on the top of a windy hill. It was Dame Tap-Tap's home. The chair flew down to her front door, outside which there was a wooden bench. The three of them pulled the snoring wizard out of the chair and put him on the bench.

Then Binky took hold of the knocker and banged it hard, four times. 'Rat-tat-tat-tat!'

He yelled at the top of his voice:

'Dame Tap-Tap! Here's a present for you!'

Then he and the children bundled into the wishing-chair again, and off they flew into the air, leaning over to see the old dame crying out in astonishment and delight when she opened the door and found the wizard Ho-ho sleeping outside!

'What a shock for him when he wakes up!' said Binky, with a grin. 'Well, children, many, many thanks for your help. You've saved Apple-pie village from a very nasty fellow. It will be nice to think of him dusting Dame Tap-Tap's kitchen, and getting water for her from the well! I guess she'll make him work hard!'

'Ho, ho!' roared the children, as the chair flew down to their playroom. 'Perhaps the wizard won't say "ho, ho" quite so much to Dame Tap-Tap!'

'No! He might get a spanking if he did,' grinned Binky. 'Well, here we are! See you tomorrow, children!'

CHAPTER 5

POOR LOST BINKY

Once a dreadful thing happened when the children were adventuring on the wishing-chair. It had grown its wings most conveniently when all three were in the playroom, so they jumped on, and were soon flying high in the air.

As they were flying they heard a loud droning noise, and looked round.

'It's an aeroplane!' shouted Peter.

'I say! It's very near us!' cried Mollie.

So it was. It didn't seem to see them at all. It flew straight at them, and the edge of one widespread wing just touched their flying chair, giving it a tremendous jerk.

Mollie and Peter were sitting tightly in the seat – but Binky was on the back, and he was jolted right off the chair.

Mollie clutched at him as he fell – but she only just touched him. The two children watched in the greatest dismay as he fell down – and down – and down.

'Oh, Peter!' cried Mollie, in despair. 'Poor, poor Binky! Whatever will happen to him!'

The aeroplane flew on steadily, never guessing that it had touched a wishing-chair. Peter turned pale and looked at Mollie.

'We must make the chair go down and see if Binky is

hurt,' he said. 'Oh dear! What a dreadful thing to happen! Chair, fly down to earth!'

The chair flapped its red wings and flew slowly down to the ground. It stood there, and the children jumped off. They were in open country with wide fields all around them. There was no sign of Binky at all.

They heard the sound of someone chanting a song, and saw coming towards them, a round, fat little man carrying a bundle on his head.

'Hi!' called Peter. 'Have you seen a little pixie falling out of the sky?'

'Is that a riddle?' said the round little man, grinning stupidly. 'I can ask *you* one too! Have you seen a horse that quacks like a duck?'

'Don't be silly,' said Mollie. 'This is serious. Our friend has fallen out of the sky.'

'Well, tell him not to do it again,' said the little round man. 'All that fell out of the sky today was a large snowflake! *Good* morning!'

He went on his way, his bundle bobbing on his head. The children were very angry.

'Making a joke about a serious thing like poor Binky falling out of the sky!' said Mollie, with tears in her eyes. 'Horrid fellow.'

'Here's someone else,' said Peter. 'Hi! Stop a minute!'

The someone was another round, fat person, also carrying a bundle on her head and singing a little song. She stopped when she saw the children.

'Have you seen a pixie falling out of the sky?' asked Peter.

'No. Have you?' said the round little woman, grinning.

'Of course!' said Mollie impatiently.

'Fibber!' said the round woman. 'A big snowflake fell out of the sky, but nothing else.'

'They've got snowflakes on the brain!' said Peter, as the woman went on her way, singing. 'Come on, Mollie. We'd better go and look for Binky ourselves. We know that it was somewhere near here that he fell. We'll carry the chair between us so that we may have it safely. I don't trust these stupid people.'

They carried the chair along and came to a marketplace. It was full of the same round, fat people, all humming and singing. A town-crier was going round the market, ringing a bell, and crying, 'Oyez! Oyez! Dame Apple-pie has lost her spectacles! Oyez! Oyez!'

Then Peter had a splendid idea. 'I say, Mollie! Let's tell the town-crier to shout out about Binky. We'll offer a reward to anyone that can tell us about him. *Someone* must have seen him fall.'

So, before very long the town-crier was ringing his bell and crying loudly, 'Oyez! Oyez! A reward is offered to anyone having news of a pixie who fell from the sky! Oyez!'

Mollie and Peter stood on a platform so that people might know to whom to go if they had news. To their delight there came quite a crowd of people to them.

'We've news, we've news!' they cried, struggling to get to Peter first.

'Well, where did you see the pixie fall?' asked Peter of the first little man.

'Sir, I saw a big snowflake fall in the Buttercup Field,' said he.

'Don't be foolish,' said Peter. 'I said a *pixie,* not a snowflake. Don't you know the difference between pixies and snowflakes? We all know that snowflakes fall from the sky. That is not news. Next, please!'

But the next person said the same thing – and the next – and the next! It was most annoying and very disappointing.

'We want our reward!' suddenly shouted someone. 'We have given you news, but you have given us no reward.'

'You haven't given us the right news!' shouted back Peter angrily.

'That doesn't matter!' shouted the little folk, looking angry. They looked rather funny too, because for some reason or other they all carried their bundles and baskets balanced on their heads. 'Give us our reward!'

They swarmed towards the platform on which the two children were standing, and Mollie and Peter suddenly felt frightened.

'I don't like this, Mollie,' said Peter. 'Let's go! These stupid creatures think that pixies and snowflakes are exactly the same – and we certainly can't give them *all* a reward. Climb into the chair!'

Mollie jumped into the chair, which was just near them on the platform. Peter sat on the arm and cried out loudly, 'Home, Chair, quickly!'

The chair flapped its wings and rose up – but it didn't rise very high, only just above the heads of the angry people. Its legs began to jerk in and out, and to Peter's enormous astonishment, the chair kicked off bundles, pots and baskets from the heads of the furious marketers! Peter began to laugh, for, really, it was most comical to see the chair playing such a trick – but Mollie was in tears.

'What's the matter?' asked Peter, drying her tears with his handkerchief.

'It's Binky,' sobbed Mollie. 'I did love him so. Now I feel we shall never see him again.'

Peter's eyes filled with tears too. 'He was such a good

friend,' he said. 'Oh, Mollie! It would be so dreadful if we never saw him again.'

They flew home in silence. The chair flew in at the playroom door and the children jumped off.

'It will never be so nice going on adventures again,' said Mollie.

'Why ever not?' said a merry little voice – and the children turned round in joy – for there was Binky, the pixie, sitting on the floor, reading a book!

'Binky! We thought you were lost for ever when you fell from the chair!' cried Mollie, hugging him hard.

'Don't break me in half!' said Binky. 'I wasn't hurt at all! I just changed myself into a big snow flake and fell into the Buttercup Field. Then I caught the next bus back to the bottom of the garden, and here I am. I've been waiting simply ages for you!'

'A snowflake!' cried Peter. 'So that's why everyone talked about snowflakes! *Now* I understand?'

He told Binky all about their adventures – and *how* the pixie laughed when he heard about the chair kicking the bundles off the heads of the angry people!

'I wish I'd been there!' he said. 'Come on, now – what about a game of ludo?'

CHAPTER 6

THE LAND OF DREAMS

'Mollie! Peter! Come quickly! The chair is growing its wings again!' whispered Binky, peeping in at the dining-room window. The children were busy drawing and painting, but they at once put away their things and scampered down the garden to their playroom.

'Goody!' cried Peter, as he saw the red wings of the chair slowly flapping to and fro. 'Come on, everyone. Where shall we go to this time?'

'We'll let the chair take us where it wants to,' said Binky, sitting on the top of the back as usual. 'Off we go – and mind you don't get worried if I fall off, Mollie!'

'Oh, I shan't worry any more!' laughed Mollie. 'You can look after yourself all right, Binky!'

Off they went into the air.

'Where's the chair going, Binky?' asked Mollie, presently.

'I think it's going to the Land of Dreams,' said Binky. 'Oh! I don't know that I like that! Strange things happen there! Perhaps we'd better not go!'

'Oh, do let's!' said Peter. '*We'll* be all right!'

Down to the Land of Dreams flew the chair and came to rest outside a small sweet shop. Peter felt in his pocket and found a penny there. 'I'll buy some toffee!' he cried. He went into the shop, and saw a large old sheep sitting there, knitting. He stared at her in surprise and then asked for a pennyworth of toffee. She gave him some in a bag and he ran out. He opened the bag and offered the toffee to the others.

But when they tried to take some they found that the bag was full of green peas! How extraordinary!

'I told you strange things happened here,' said Binky. 'Come on. Let's carry the chair in case it runs away or something!' He turned to pick it up, and gave a shout!

It had turned into a little dog, and its red wings were now red ribbons round the dog's neck!

'I say! Look at that! What are we going to do now?' said Binky in dismay. They all stared at the dog, which wagged its tail hard.

Suddenly there came an angry shout behind them.

'Spot! Spot! Come here, sir!'

The children turned and saw a clown running down the road, calling to the dog.

'Quick! We must run off with the dog before the clown gets it,' said Binky. 'It may change back into a chair again at any moment, and we can't let anyone else have it.'

He caught up the surprised dog, and the three of them raced down the street at top speed.

'Stop thief, stop thief!' shouted the clown, and ran after them. He caught them up and took hold of Binky. To the children's amazement the clown then turned into a large fat policeman!

'I arrest you for stealing a dog!' said the policeman
solemnly. Binky stared at him in despair. But Mollie cried
out loudly: 'What do you mean, policeman? We haven't
any dog!'

And sure enough the dog had changed into a yellow
duck! There it was, under Binky's arm, quacking away for
all it was worth! The policeman stared at it, looked very
blue, and in a trice had changed into a blue motor-van
that trundled itself down the street!

'I don't like this land,' said Mollie. 'Things are never the
same two minutes running!'

'Nor are they in dreams!' said Binky. 'You can't expect
anything else here. I didn't want to come, you know. I say,
won't one of you carry this duck? It's awfully heavy.'

He handed it to Peter, a great yellow bird – but even

as Peter took it, something strange happened! The bird's beak, legs and tail disappeared, and all that was left was a great pile of yellow stuff that slithered about in Peter's hands!

'Ow!' he cried. 'It's cold! It's ice-cream! I can't hold it!'

'You must, you must!' shouted Binky, and he and Mollie did their best to hold the slippery mass together. But it was no good – it slithered to the ground and began to melt!

'There goes our chair!' said Binky sorrowfully. 'It looks as if we are here for ever now! First it turned into a dog, then into a duck, and now into ice-cream! This is a horrid adventure!'

They left the melting ice-cream and went on down the street. Peter took out his bag of green peas and looked at them again. They had turned into tiny balloons, ready

to be blown up. He gave one to Binky and one to Mollie. They began to blow them up – but, oh dear, dear, dear! instead of blowing up the balloons, they blew themselves up! Yes, they really did! Peter stared in dismay, but he couldn't stop them! There they were, Mollie and Binky, two big balloons swaying about in the air – and they even had strings tied to them! Peter was afraid they might blow away, so he took hold of the strings.

He wandered down the street alone, very puzzled and unhappy. Nothing seemed real. The Land of Dreams was very peculiar indeed! The two enormous balloons floated along behind him, and when he turned to look at them what a shock he had!

They were not in the least like Binky and Mollie any more! One was green and one was blue – and even as Peter stared at them, the air began to escape from each balloon! They rapidly grew smaller – and smaller – and smaller – and soon they were just tiny lumps of coloured rubber, hanging from the string. Peter looked at them sadly.

'All that's left of Mollie and Binky!' he thought unhappily. 'No wishing-chair either! Only me! Oh dear, oh dear! Whatever will be the end of this strange adventure?'

He put the balloons into his pocket, and went on. He came to a large hall, where a concert seemed to be going on. He slipped inside and sat down on a chair. He suddenly felt very tired indeed. He shut his eyes and yawned.

The chair began to rock softly. Peter opened his eyes, and saw that it had changed into a rocking-horse! But things no longer astonished him in the Land of Dreams.

It would be surprising if peculiar things *didn't* happen, not if they did!

Soon he was fast asleep on the rocking-horse. It rose up into the air and flew out of the door. Peter slept on. He didn't wake up until hours afterwards, and when at last he opened his eyes, what a surprise!

He was in the playroom at home, lying on the rug by the window! He sat up at once, and remembered everything. Sorrowfully he put his hands into his pockets and pulled out the two air balloons.

'Mollie and Binky!' said Peter sadly.

'Yes! Do you want us?' said Mollie's voice, and to his astonishment and delight he saw both Mollie and Binky sitting in the wishing-chair nearby, both yawning, just waking up from a sleep.

'Oh!' he said. 'I must have dreamt it all then! Listen, you two! I had such a funny dream! I went to the Land of Dreams and –'

'Yes, yes, yes!' said Binky impatiently. 'We've all been there. It was a real adventure. I don't want to go there again. Ooooh! It was a horrid feeling turning into a balloon! It was a good thing you put us into your pocket, Peter!'

'Was it a *real* adventure then?' cried Peter, in amazement.

'As real as adventures ever are in the Land of Dreams,' said Binky. 'Now, what about some *real* toffee – that won't turn into green peas or balloons? Get some treacle from your cook, Mollie, and we'll make some. We deserve a treat after that horrid adventure!'

CHAPTER 7
THE RUNAWAY CHAIR

One morning, when the two children went down to their playroom to have a game with Binky the pixie, they found him fast asleep.

'Wake up!' cried Peter, rolling him over. But Binky didn't wake up! He was breathing very deeply, and had quite nice, red cheeks – but he simply would *not* wake up!

'What's the matter with him?' said Mollie, puzzled.

'Oh, he's just pretending,' said Peter. 'I'll get a wet sponge! He'll soon wake then!'

But even the sponge didn't wake him up.

'There must be a spell on him or something,' said Mollie, rather frightened. 'What shall we do, Peter? If only we knew where to get help. But we mustn't tell anyone about Binky – he'd be so cross when he woke up. And we don't know how to find any fairies, or we could ask *them* for help!'

Suddenly the wishing-chair gave a creak, and Mollie looked round. 'It's growing its wings!' she cried. 'Don't let it fly away, Peter! We don't want an adventure without Binky!'

Peter ran to the chair – but it dodged him and flew straight out of the door, its wings flapping swiftly. Peter stared after it in dismay.

'Oh, Peter!' said Mollie. 'Isn't this dreadful! Here's Binky under a spell, or something – and now the chair's run away! What an unlucky day!'

'Well, it's gone,' said Peter gloomily. 'Now what *are* we going to do about Binky, Mollie?'

Just then there came the sound of a cautious tiptoe noise. Peter turned – just in time to see an ugly goblin slipping out of the door! 'I put him under the sleepy spell!' shouted the goblin. 'I meant to steal the chair before he woke up – but *you* came! Now I'm going to find the chair! If you don't find the way to wake up that pixie before twelve o'clock tonight, he will vanish altogether! Ho, ho!'

'Horrid thing!' said Mollie, as the goblin disappeared into the garden. 'I suppose he will go after our chair and have it for himself – and here he's left Binky in a magic sleep and we don't know how to wake him! If only, only, only we knew how to find a fairy who might help us!'

'I'll go and call for one in the garden,' said Peter. So he went out and called softly here and there. 'Fairies! If you are there, come and help me!'

But he had no answer at all, and he went sadly back to the playroom where Mollie sat by the sleeping pixie.

'No good,' said Peter. 'I didn't see a single fairy. I really don't know what we are to do!'

'If only we had the chair we could go off in it and find a fairy somewhere to help us,' said Mollie. 'But even that's gone and left us – run away on the very day we needed its help!'

They went back to the house for dinner and for tea, and

43

Mother exclaimed at their long faces. They very nearly told her about Binky, but didn't like to, for they had solemnly promised the pixie never to mention his name to the grown-ups.

When it was their bedtime, Binky was still asleep!

'Fancy! He hasn't had anything to eat all day!' said Mollie. 'Oh, Peter, do you really think he will disappear at midnight, if we can't wake him up?'

'We *must* wake him!' said Peter. So he got two drums and two trumpets, and he and Mollie made as much noise as ever they could until Jane, the housemaid, was sent down the garden to stop them. But Binky didn't even stir in his sleep!

Then they poured cold water down his neck – but that only made him wet, and didn't make him flicker so much as an eyelash! Then they found a hen's feather, set it alight, and let it smoulder just under the pixie's nose – but the strong smell did not even make him turn away. He slept on peacefully.

A bell rang in the distance.

'Oh dear! There's our bedtime bell!' said Mollie, in dismay. 'Peter, I'm coming back to the playroom tonight, somehow. There surely must be something we can do!'

'We've tried everything!' said Peter, and looked very miserable. They went off to bed, first covering up Binky warmly. In an hour's time they were back again, in their dressing-gowns! They had slipped out of bed, run out of the garden door, and gone to the playroom without being seen!

Binky was still fast asleep. Mollie looked at the clock. 'Half-past eight!' she said. 'Oh dear!'

They tried to think of more ways to waken up the sleeping pixie, and Mollie squeezed a sponge over his head with icy-cold water, and then with hot water – but neither had any effect at all. The hands of the clock stole round and round – and at last it was only ten minutes to midnight. The children were quite in despair.

Suddenly there came a curious sound of knocking at the door. It sounded more like kicking. Peter ran to it. Outside was their wishing-chair, wet through, for it was raining! It had found the door shut and had kicked at it with one of its front legs. Sitting in it was a jolly-faced gnome with a silvery beard and enormous nose, two pairs of spectacles and a large umbrella to keep off the rain.

'Who are you?' said Peter, in surprise.

'Oh, don't bother him with questions!' said Mollie

anxiously. 'He's a fairy of some sort. Perhaps he has come to make Binky better.'

'Yes,' said the gnome, putting on a third pair of spectacles. 'This chair knew where I lived, and flew one hundred and thirty-three miles to fetch me! I am only just in time.'

'There are only seven minutes till midnight,' said Mollie. 'Do be quick!'

The little gnome doctor rolled up his sleeves, took a towel and a piece of soap from the air, and with them washed Binky's face very carefully. Then he brushed the sleeping pixie's eyes with a peacock's feather that he also took most conveniently from the air, and smeared them with a peculiar-smelling yellow ointment.

'Do hurry!' said Mollie. 'It's almost midnight. The clock's going to strike!'

'It's one minute fast,' said the doctor. He took a black ball from the air, opened it, put a blue powder inside it, struck a match, and put it to the black ball. At once there was a loud explosion and the playroom rocked and shook. Smoke covered the room. It had a very pleasant smell. When it cleared, the two children saw, to their delight, that Binky was sitting up, looking most astonished.

'Who made that horrible noise?' he said crossly. 'Hallo, doctor! What are *you* doing here?'

'Just going, so goodbye!' grinned the little gnome. 'See you some day!'

He jumped into the wishing-chair, which at once flew off with him again. Binky ran his finger round his collar and frowned.

46

'Who's been wetting me?' he asked.

'Oh, Binky, don't be cross!' begged Mollie. 'We've been quite anxious about you. A goblin put you under a sleepy-spell – and the clever wishing-chair went to fetch that gnome doctor you saw – only just in time too!'

'So *that's* it, is it!' said Binky. 'No wonder I feel so hungry. I've been asleep all day, I suppose. Can you find me anything to eat?'

'There are some buns and apples in the cupboard,' said Peter, delighted to see Binky awake again: 'We'll have a fine feast!'

So they did – and they didn't go back to bed till the cock crew! No wonder they slept late the next morning. Binky didn't, though! He was up bright and early. He had quite enough of sleeping!

CHAPTER 8

THE LOST CAT

One morning it was very wet, and Mollie, Peter and Binky were playing a very noisy game of snap in the playroom together. Whiskers, the cat, had come with them and had curled herself up on a cushion in the wishing-chair, where she had gone fast asleep.

'Snap! Snap! SNAP!' yelled the children – and were so interested in their game that they didn't hear a little flapping sound. The wishing-chair had grown its wings and was flapping them gently to and fro. Before anyone noticed the chair rose silently into the air and flew out of the open door – taking the puss-cat with it, still fast asleep!

'Snap!' yelled Binky, and took the last pile of cards in glee. 'I've won!'

'Good,' said Peter. He looked round the playroom to see what game to play next – and then he looked rather surprised and scared.

'I say!' he said. 'Where's the chair gone?'

Binky and Mollie looked round too. Mollie went pale.

'It's gone!' she said.

'It was here when we began our game,' said Binky. 'It must have slipped out without us noticing. I sort of remember feeling a little draught. It must have been its wings flapping.'

'Whiskers has gone too!' said Mollie, in alarm. 'She was asleep on the cushion. Oh, Binky – will she come back?'

'Depends where she has gone to,' said Binky. 'She's a black cat, you know – and if a witch should see her she might take her to help in her spells. Black cats are clever with spells.'

Mollie began to cry. She was very fond of Whiskers. 'Oh, why did we let Whiskers go to sleep on that chair?' she wept.

'Well, it's no good crying,' said Binky, patting Mollie's shoulder. 'We must just wait and see. Perhaps old Whiskers will come back still fast asleep when the chair returns!'

They waited for an hour or two with the door wide open – but no wishing-chair came back. The two children left Binky and went to their dinner. They hunted about the house just in case Whiskers should have got off the chair cushion and wandered home – but no one had seen her.

After dinner they ran down the garden to their playroom again. Binky was there, looking gloomy.

'The chair hasn't come back,' he said.

But, just as he spoke, Peter gave a shout and pointed up into the sky. There was the chair, flapping its way back, all its red wings twinkling up and down.

'Look! There's the chair! Oh, I do hope Whiskers is on her cushion. Suppose she has fallen out!'

The chair flapped its way downwards, and flew in at the open door. It came to rest in its usual place and gave a sigh and a creak. The children rushed to it.

There was no cat there! The cushion was still in its place, with a dent in the middle where Whiskers had lain – but that was all!

The three stared at one another in dismay.

'Whiskers has been caught by a witch,' said Binky. 'There's no doubt about it. Look at this!'

He picked up a tiny silver star that lay on the seat of the chair. 'This little star has fallen off a witch's embroidered cloak.'

'Poor Whiskers!' wept Mollie. 'I do want her back. Oh, Binky, what shall we do?'

'Well, we'd better find out first where she's gone,' said Binky. 'Then, the next time the chair grows its wings we'll go and rescue her.'

'How can we find out where she's gone?' asked Mollie, drying her eyes.

'I'll have to work a spell to find that out,' said Binky. 'I'll have to get a few pixies in to help me. Go and sit down on the couch, Mollie and Peter, and don't speak a word until I've finished. The pixies won't help me if you interfere. They are very shy just about here.'

Mollie and Peter did as they were told. They sat down on the couch feeling rather excited. Binky went to the open door and clapped his hands softly three times, then loudly seven times. He whistled like a blackbird, and then called a magic word that sounded like 'Looma, looma, looma, loo.'

In a minute or two four little pixies, a bit smaller than Binky, who was himself a pixie, came running in at the door. They stopped when they saw the two children, but Binky said they were his friends.

'They won't interfere,' he said. 'I want to do a spell to find out where this wishing-chair has just been to. Will you help me?'

The pixies twittered like swallows and nodded their heads. Binky sat down in the wishing-chair, holding in his hands a mirror that he had borrowed from Mollie. The four little pixies joined hands and danced round the chair, first one way and then another, chanting a magic song that got higher and higher and quicker and quicker as they danced round in time to their singing.

Binky looked intently into the mirror, and the children watched, wondering what he would see there.

Suddenly the four dancing pixies stopped their singing and fell to the floor, panting and crying, 'Now look and tell what you see, Binky!'

Binky stared into the mirror and then gave a shout.

'I see her! It's the witch Kirri-Kirri! *She* has got Whiskers. Here she is, cooking her dinner for her!'

The two children sprang up from the couch and hurried to look into the mirror that Binky held. To their great amazement, instead of seeing their own faces, they saw a picture of Whiskers, their cat, stirring a soup-pot on a big stove – and behind her was an old witch, clad in a long, black cloak embroidered with silver stars and moons!

'See her!' said Binky, pointing. 'That's the witch Kirri-Kirri. I know where she lives. We'll go and rescue Whiskers this very night – even if we have to go on foot!'

The four little pixies twittered goodbye and ran out. The picture in the mirror faded away. The children and the pixie looked at one another.

'What a marvellous spell!' said Mollie. 'Oh, I did enjoy that, Binky! Shall we really go and fetch Whiskers tonight?'

'Yes,' said Binky. 'Come here at midnight, ready dressed. If the chair has grown its wings, we'll go in it – if not, we'll take the underground train to the witch's house.'

'Ooh!' said Mollie. 'What an adventure!'

CHAPTER 9
THE WITCH KIRRI-KIRRI

The children dressed themselves again after they had been to bed and slept. Mollie had a little alarm-clock and she set it for a quarter to twelve, so they awoke in good time for their adventure. Binky was waiting for them.

'We can't go in the wishing-chair,' he said. 'It hasn't grown its wings again. I think it's asleep, because it gave a tiny snore just now!'

'How funny!' said Mollie. 'Oh, Binky – I do feel excited!'

'Come on,' said the pixie. 'There's no time to lose if we want to catch the underground train.'

He led the children to a big tree at the bottom of the garden. He twisted a piece of the bark and a door slid open. There was a narrow stairway in the tree going downwards. Mollie and Peter were so surprised to see it.

'Go down the stairs,' Binky said to them. 'I'll just shut the door behind us.'

They climbed down and came to a small passage. Binky joined them and they went along it until they came to a big turnstile, where a solemn grey rabbit sat holding a bundle of tickets.

'We want tickets for Witch Kirri-Kirri's,' said Binky. The

rabbit gave them three yellow tickets and let them through the turnstile. There was a little platform beyond with a railway line running by it. Almost at once a train appeared out of the darkness. Its lamps gleamed like two eyes. There were no carriages – just open trucks with cushions in. The train was very crowded, and the children and Binky found it difficult to get seats.

Gnomes, brownies, rabbits, moles, elves and hedge-hogs sat in the trucks, chattering and laughing. The two hedgehogs had a truck to themselves for they were so prickly that no one wanted to sit by them.

The train set off with much clattering. It stopped at station after station, and at last came to one labelled 'Kirri-Kirri Station'.

Binky and the children got out.

'Kirri-Kirri is such a rich and powerful witch that she has a station of her own,' explained Binky. 'Now listen – this is my plan, children. It's no use us asking the witch for Whiskers, our cat – she just won't let us have her. And it's no use trying to get her by magic, because the witch's magic is much stronger than mine. We must get her by a trick.'

'What trick?' asked the children.

'We'll creep into her little garden,' said Binky, 'and we'll make scrapey noises on the wall, like mice. We'll squeak like mice too – and the witch will hear us and send Whiskers out to catch the mice. Then we'll get her, run back to the station, and catch the next train home!'

'What a fine plan!' said Peter. 'It's so simple too! It can't go wrong!'

'Sh!' said Binky, pointing to a large house in the

distance. 'That's Kirri-Kirri's house.'

They had left the station behind and had come up into the open air again. The moonlight was bright enough to show them the road, and they could see everything very clearly indeed.

They slipped inside the witch's wicket-gate. 'You go to that end of the house and I'll go to the other,' said Binky. So Peter and Mollie crept to one end and began to scratch against the wall with bits of stick, whilst Binky did the same the other end. Then they squeaked as high as they could, exactly like mice.

They heard a window being thrown up, and saw the witch's head outlined against the lamplight.

'Mice again!' she grumbled. 'Hie, Whiskers, come here! Catch them, catch them!'

Whiskers jumped down into the garden. The witch slammed down the window and drew the blind. Mollie made a dash for the big black cat and lifted her into her arms. Whiskers purred nineteen to the dozen and rubbed her soft head against Mollie's hand. Binky and Peter came up in delight.

'The plan worked beautifully!' said Peter. 'Come on – let's go to the station!'

And then a most unfortunate thing happened! Peter fell over a bush and came down with a loud clatter on the path! At once the window flew up again and Kirri-Kirri looked out. She shouted a very magic word and slammed the window down again.

'Oh dear, oh dear, oh dear!' groaned Binky at once.

'What's the matter?' asked Mollie, scared.

'She's put a spell round the garden!' said the pixie. 'We can't get out! She'll find us here in the morning!'

'Can't get out!' said Peter, going to the gate. 'What nonsense! *I'm* going, anyway!'

But although he opened the gate he couldn't walk out. It was as if there was an invisible wall all round the garden! The children couldn't get out anywhere. They forced their way through the hedge – but still the invisible wall seemed to be just beyond, and there was no way of getting out at all!

'Whatever shall we do?' asked Mollie.

'We can't do anything,' said Binky gloomily. 'Peter was an awful silly to go and fall over like that, just when we had done everything so well.'

'I'm terribly sorry,' said poor Peter. 'I do wish I hadn't.

I didn't mean to.'

'Well, we'd better go and sit down in the porch,' said Binky, who was shivering. 'It's warmer there.'

They sat huddled together in the porch and Mollie took Whiskers on her knee, saying she would make a nice hot-water bottle.

They were nodding off to sleep, for they were all very tired, when Whiskers suddenly began to snarl and spit. The children and Binky woke up in a fright. They saw something flying round the garden, like a big black bird! Mollie stared – and then she leapt up and whispered as loudly as she dared – 'It isn't a bird! It's the dear old wishing-chair! It's come to find us!'

Binky gave a chuckle of delight. He ran to the chair and took hold of it.

'Come on!' he said to the others. 'The only way out of this bewitched garden is by flying up and up. We can't get out any other way! The wishing-chair is just what we want!'

They all got into the chair. Whiskers was on Mollie's knee. The chair flapped its wings, rose up into the air and flew almost to the clouds!

'What will old Kirri-Kirri say in the morning when she finds *no* one in her garden, not even Whiskers!' giggled Binky. 'She'll think she's been dreaming! I wish I could see her face!'

The chair flew to the playroom. The children said goodnight to Binky, and, with Whiskers in her arms, Mollie ran with Peter up the path to their house. They were soon in bed and asleep. As for Whiskers, you may be sure she never went to sleep in the wishing-chair again!

CHAPTER 10

THE DISAPPEARING ISLAND

It happened once that the children and Binky had a most unpleasant adventure, and it was all Mollie's fault.

The wishing-chair grew its wings one bright sunny morning just as the three of them were planning a game of pirates. Mollie saw the red wings growing from the legs of the chair and cried out in delight.

'Look! The chair's off again! Let's get in and have an adventure!'

They all crowded into it, and in a trice the chair was off through the door and into the air. It was such fun, for the day was clear and sunny, and the children could see for miles.

The chair flew on and on, and came to the towers and spires of Fairyland. They glittered in the sun and Peter wanted to go down and visit the prince and princess they had once rescued. But the chair still flew on. It flew over the Land of Gnomes, and over the Land of Toadstools, and at last came to a bright blue sea.

'Hallo, hallo!' said Binky, peering over the edge of the chair. 'I've never been as far as this before. I don't know if we ought to fly over the sea. The chair might get tired – and then what would happen to us if we all came down in the sea!'

'We shan't do that!' said Mollie, pointing to a blue island far away on the horizon. 'I think the chair is making for that land over there.'

The chair flew steadily towards it, and the children saw that the land they had seen in the distance was a small and beautiful island. It was packed with flowers, and the sound of bells came faintly up from the fields and hills.

'We mustn't go there,' said Binky suddenly. 'That's Disappearing Island!'

'Well, why shouldn't we go there?' said Mollie.

'Because it suddenly disappears,' said Binky. 'I've heard of it before. It's a horrid place. You get there and think it's all as beautiful as can be – and then it suddenly disappears and takes you with it.'

'It can't be horrid,' said Mollie longingly, looking down at the sunny, flower-spread island. 'Oh, Binky, you must be mistaken. It's the most beautiful island I ever saw! I do want to go. There are some lovely birds there too. I can hear them singing.'

'I tell you, Mollie, it's dangerous to go to Disappearing Island,' said Binky crossly. 'You might believe me.'

'You're not always right!' said Mollie obstinately. 'I *want* to go there! Wishing-chair, fly down to that lovely island.'

At once the chair began to fly downwards. Binky glared at Mollie, but the words were said. He couldn't unsay them. Down they flew and down and down!

The brilliant island came nearer and nearer. Mollie shouted in delight to see such glorious bright flowers, such shiny-winged birds, such plump, soft rabbits. The chair flew swiftly towards them.

And then, just as they were about to land in a field spread with buttercups as large as poppies, among soft-eyed bunnies and singing birds, a most strange and peculiar thing happened.

The island disappeared! One moment it was there, and the sun was shining on its fields – and the next moment there was only a faint blue mist! The chair flew through the mist – and then SPLASH! They were all in the sea!

Mollie and Peter were flung off the chair into the water. Binky grabbed the back of the chair, and reached his hand out to the children. They clambered back on to the chair, which was bobbing about on the waves, soaking wet.

'What did I tell you?' said Binky angrily. 'Didn't I say it was Disappearing Island? Now see what's happened! It's gone and disappeared, and we've fallen into the sea! A nice pickle we are in – all wet and shivery! Just like a girl to get us into this mess!'

Mollie went red. How she wished she hadn't wanted to go to Disappearing Island!

'Well, I didn't know it was going to disappear so suddenly,' she said. 'I'm very sorry.'

'Not much good being sorry,' said Peter gloomily, squeezing the water out of his clothes. 'How are we going to get to land? As far as I can see there is water all round us for miles! The chair's wings are wet, and it can't fly.'

The three of them were indeed in a dreadful fix! It was fortunate for them that the chair was made of wood, or they would not have had anything to cling to!

They bobbed up and down for some time, wondering what to do. Suddenly, to their great surprise, a little head popped out of the sea.

'Hallo!' it said. 'Are you wanting help?'

'Yes,' said Binky. 'Are you a merman?'

'I am!' said the little fellow. The children looked down at him, and through the green water they could see his fish-like body covered with scales from the waist downwards and ending in a silvery tail. 'Do you want to be towed to land?'

'Yes, please,' said Binky joyfully.

'That will cost you a piece of gold,' said the merman.

'I haven't any with me, but we will send it to you as soon as we get home,' promised Binky. The merman swam off and came back riding on a big fish. He threw a rope of seaweed around the back of the chair and shouted to Binky to hold on to it. Then the fish set off at a great speed, towing the chair behind it with Binky and the children safely on it! The merman rode on the fish all the way, singing a funny little watery song. It was a strange ride!

Soon they came to land, and the children dragged the chair out of the water on to the sunbaked sand. 'Thank you,' they said to the merman. 'We will send you the money as soon as we can.'

The merman jumped on the fish again, waved his wet hand, and dived into the waves with a splash.

'We'll wait till the sun has dried the chair's wings, and we'll dry our own clothes,' said Binky. 'Then we'll go home. I think that was a most unpleasant adventure. We might have been bobbing about for days on the sea!'

Mollie didn't say anything. She knew it was all her fault. They dried their clothes, and as soon as the wings of the chair were quite dry too, they sat in it, and Binky cried, 'Home, wishing-chair, home!'

They flew home. Mollie jumped off the chair as soon as it arrived in the playroom and ran to her money-box. She tipped out all her money.

'Here you are, Binky,' she said. 'I'm going to pay for that fish-ride myself. It was all my fault. I'm very sorry, and I won't be so silly again. Do forgive me!'

'Oh! That's very nice of you, Mollie!' said Binky, and he gave her a hug. 'Of course we forgive you! All's well that ends well! We're home again safe and sound!'

He changed Mollie's money into a big gold piece and gave it to the blackbird in the garden, asking him to take it to the merman.

'That's the end of *that* adventure!' said Binky. 'Well, let's hope our next one will be much, much nicer!'

CHAPTER 11
THE MAGICIAN'S PARTY

One afternoon, when the children and Binky were reading stories, there came a timid knock at the door. 'Come in!' called Mollie. The door opened and in came two small elves.

'May we speak to Binky?' they asked. Binky waved them to a chair.

'Sit down,' he said. 'What do you want?'

'Please, may we borrow your wishing-chair to go to the Magician Greatheart's party,' said the bigger elf.

'Well, it doesn't belong to me,' said Binky. 'It belongs to these two children.'

'Would you let us borrow it?' asked the little elves.

'Certainly,' said Mollie and Peter.

'What reward do you ask?' said the elves.

'Oh, you can have the chair for nothing,' said Mollie. 'Bring it back safely, that's all.'

'I suppose you wouldn't like to come to the party?' asked the elves. 'We are very small, and there are only five of us to go. There would be plenty of room for you and for Binky too in the chair.'

'Stars and moon, what a treat!' cried Binky in delight. 'Yes, we'll all go! Thanks very much! Greatheart's parties are glorious! My word, this *is* luck! When is the party, elves?'

'Tomorrow night,' said the elves. 'Sharp at midnight. We'll be here at half-past eleven.'

'Right,' said Binky. The little elves said goodbye and ran out. Binky rubbed his hands and turned to the two delighted children.

'The magician is a marvellous fellow,' he said. 'He is a good magician, and the enchantments and magic he knows are perfectly wonderful. I hope he does a few tricks! Put on your best clothes and be here at half-past eleven tomorrow night, won't you!'

The children were most excited. They talked about nothing else all day long and the next day too. They dressed themselves in their best clothes and ran down to

silver stick and tapped three times on the floor. A spire of green smoke came up and made a crackling noise. It shot up into the air, turned over and over and wound its way among the guests, dropping tiny bunches of sweet-smelling flowers as it passed – buttonholes for everyone!

The smoke went. The magician tapped the floor again and up rose five black cats, each with a violin except the last one, and he had a drum. After the cats came six plump rabbits, who danced to the tunes that the cats played. One rabbit turned upside down and danced on his ears, and that made Peter laugh so much that he had to get out his handkerchief to wipe his tears of laughter away.

Then an even stranger thing happened next. The magician tapped the floor once more, and up came a great flower of yellow. It opened, and in the middle of it the guests could see five red eggs. The eggs broke and out came tiny chicks. They grew – and grew – and grew – and became great brilliant birds with long drooping tails. Then they opened their beaks and sang so sweetly that not a sound could be heard in the great hall but their voices.

The birds flew away. The flower faded. The magician tapped the floor for the last time. A gnome appeared, whose long beard floated round him like a mist. He handed Greatheart a big dish with a lid. The magician took off the lid and lifted out a silver spoon. He stirred in the air and a bubbling sound came. Round the spoon grew a glass bowl. The children could see the spoon shining in it. But suddenly the spoon turned to gold and swam about – a live goldfish.

Greatheart took the goldfish neatly into his hand and

threw it into the air. It disappeared.

'Who has it?' asked Greatheart. Everyone looked about – but no one had the fish. Greatheart laughed and went over to Mollie. He put his hand into her right ear and pulled out the goldfish! Then he took up Peter's hand and opened it – and will you believe it, Peter had a little yellow chick there, cheeping away merrily!

Oh, the tricks that the magician did! No one would ever believe them! Peter and Mollie rubbed their eyes several times and wondered if they were dreaming.

Best of all came the last trick. The magician, as he said goodnight to his guests, gave each a tiny egg.

'It will hatch tomorrow,' he said. 'Keep it safely!' The children thanked him very much for a marvellous evening, and then got sleepily into the wishing-chair with Binky and the elves. How they got home they never knew – for there must have been magic about that took them home, undressed them, and popped them into bed without their knowing. Anyway, they found themselves there the next morning when they awoke, although they did not remember at all how they got there!

'I believe it was all a beautiful dream,' said Mollie.

'It wasn't!' said Peter, putting his hand under his pillow. He brought out his little egg. As he looked at it, it broke – and there, in his hand, was a tiny silver watch, ticking away merrily!

Mollie gave a scream of delight and put her hand under her pillow to get her egg too. It broke in her hand – and out of it came a necklace of beads that looked exactly like bubbles! It was the loveliest one Mollie had ever seen!

'Hurry up and dress and we'll see what Binky got,' said Mollie. They hurried – and when they saw Binky, he showed them *his* present – golden buckles for his shoes. Didn't they look grand!

'That was the loveliest party I've ever been to!' said Mollie happily. 'I wish *all* our wishing-chair adventures were like that!'

CHAPTER 12

THE WISHING-CHAIR IS FOOLISH

Once the wishing-chair was very foolish, and nearly landed the children and Binky in a dreadful fix!

It grew its wings one morning when the children were playing snakes and ladders. Binky saw the red wings flapping and jumped up in excitement.

'Come on!' he cried. 'I'm longing for another adventure!'

They all jumped on to the chair. It flew out of the door in a great hurry, and then up into the air. It was a beautiful day and the children and Binky could see for miles. The chair seemed in a rather silly mood. It swung to and fro as it flew, and even jiggled about once or twice.

'I say!' said Binky. 'I don't like this! Hold on tightly, children, in case the chair turns head-over-heels, or something silly. It's in a dangerous mood.'

'Shall we go back home?' asked Mollie, in alarm.

'Of course not!' said Peter. 'We'll never turn our backs on an adventure!'

So on they went, the chair still doing its little tricks. At last Binky really did get a bit frightened, for once Peter nearly fell off.

'Go down to earth at once, Chair!' he commanded. The chair seemed cross. It didn't want to go down – but it had to. So down it went, jiggling every now and again as if it really did mean to jerk the children off.

Peter looked down to see where they were going. There was a village below them, and they seemed to be going down towards the roof of a house.

'Hope the chair doesn't land on the roof!' said Peter. 'It looks just as if it's going to!'

But it did something even worse than land on the roof! What do you suppose it did?

It tried to go down the large red chimney belonging to the house! It really *was* behaving very foolishly!

Of course, it couldn't possibly go down – and it stuck fast, three legs in, and one out, and there it was, all sideways, with the children getting covered with soot and smoke!

Binky climbed out first, and helped Peter and Mollie out too.

They sat on the roof, holding on to the chimney, which felt rather hot, because warm smoke was coming out of it.

Binky was very angry.

'I never thought the chair would be so silly!' he said. 'It has acted so sensibly up to now. Now look what it's done! It's gone and stuck itself in somebody's chimney, and goodness knows how we're going to get it out! And here we are up on a roof in a village we don't know!'

'It's too bad,' said Mollie. 'Look at my frock! All over soot.'

'We'd better shout and see if someone will get us down,' said Peter. So they shouted.

'Hie, hie, hie! Help! Hie, hie, hie!'

Soon a gnome heard their shouting, and came out to see what it was all about. When he saw the three children up on the roof and the chair in the chimney he was amazed. He shouted to his friends, and soon the whole village was staring upwards.

'Get a ladder and help us down!' shouted Peter. 'Our chair has landed us in this fix!'

In a few minutes a long ladder was brought, and the children and Binky climbed carefully down it to the ground. Binky explained what had happened, and the village folk exclaimed in astonishment.

'The thing is,' said Peter, '*how* are we going to get the chair out? It can't stay there for the rest of its life, cooking in a chimney pot! Who would have thought it would have been so silly?'

'It's trying to get out!' said Mollie suddenly. 'Look, it's wriggling!'

So it was. It did look funny! It tried its hardest to get out, but it was stuck much too tightly.

'It's no good,' said Peter gloomily. 'It will have to stay there. I don't see how we can possibly get it out.'

'Of course we can!' said Binky. 'We'll get the village sweep to come along and put his long brush up the chimney! Then the silly old chair will be swept out of the chimney! We will get into it when it comes to earth, and go home immediately before it has time to do anything silly again!'

'I'll fetch the sweep!' said a round-faced gnome at once. 'He lives next door to me.'

He ran off, and in a few minutes came back with a little sweep, looking rather black, carrying his bundle of poles. He stared in astonishment at the chair in the chimney.

'Can you push it out for us?' asked Binky anxiously.

'I'll try,' said the sweep. He went into the house and fitted the big round brush on to the first pole. He pushed it up the chimney. Then he fitted another pole on to the first one, and pushed that up the chimney too. So he went on until the brush was almost at the top. Then he fitted on his last pole, and prepared to give a good push.

Binky, Mollie and Peter were outside the house, watching the chair in the chimney. All the gnome villagers were with them too. It was really rather exciting.

The chair gave a jolt!

'The sweep is pushing it!' yelled Binky, dancing about excitedly. 'Ooh, look! He's pushing it hard – the chair is coming out! It's nearly out!'

So it was! The sweep was pushing and pushing with his round brush, and the chair was getting loose as it was jerked farther up. Suddenly it came right out of the chimney with a rush! The sweep's brush came out too, and twiddled round in the air in a funny manner.

'There it comes, there it comes!' shouted Mollie. 'Hie, Chair, come to earth!'

But to the children's dismay, that naughty wishing-chair flapped its red wings and flew right up into the air! It didn't go *near* the ground!

'Oh, I say!' said Binky. '*Isn't* it behaving badly!'

They all watched it fly away till they could no longer see it. It was gone!

'Well,' said Mollie, 'we'll have to get home another way, that's all. I'm afraid we've lost the chair now.'

'We'll catch the bus that leaves here in five minutes' time,' said Binky, looking at a bus timetable set out on a wall nearby. 'It won't be long before we're home.'

'I'm sorry about the chair,' said Peter sadly. 'It gave us some fine adventures, you know. It has behaved very badly today, it's true – but once or twice it has been very good to us – like when it fetched us from Witch Kirri-Kirri's.'

'Yes,' said Binky, 'We mustn't forget the good things just because it has once been bad. Come on – here's the bus.'

They got into the bus, which was very peculiar,

because the driver was a duck and the conductor a rabbit. However, Binky didn't seem surprised, so Mollie and Peter said nothing, but just stared. In ten minutes they found themselves outside a cave in a hillside.

'This is where we get off,' said Binky, much to their surprise. They followed him into the cave and up some steps. Binky opened a door – and to the children's amazement they found themselves climbing out of a tree in the wood near to their home!

'You simply never know where an entrance to Fairyland is!' said Mollie, staring at the tree, as Binky shut the bark door.

They ran home – and the very first thing they saw in their playroom was – guess! Yes, their wishing-chair. They stared in astonishment.

'Why, it's come back home after all!' said Peter, delighted. 'It's wings have gone. Oh, fancy, it's come back to us! Isn't that lovely!'

'Good old chair!' said Mollie, running to it and sitting down in it. 'I'm glad it's back. I expect it's sorry now. I don't mind having nearly gone down a chimney now it's all over – it's so exciting to think of!'

'Don't say things like that in front of the chair,' said Binky. 'There's no knowing what it might do next.'

'Let's brush our clothes clean,' said Peter, getting a brush. 'We'll get into trouble if we don't – and certainly no one would believe us if we said we'd been stuck in a chimney!'

'Whatever shall we do *next*?' said Mollie. Aha! Wait and see!

CHAPTER 13
THE POLITE GOBLIN

The next time the chair grew its wings again, Binky looked at it sternly.

'Last time you were very badly behaved!' he said. 'If you want us to come with you this time, just behave yourself. If not, I'll sell you to the Jumble-Man, and you won't like that!'

The chair flapped its wings violently, and Binky grinned at the others. 'That will make it behave itself this time,' he said. 'It wouldn't like to be given to the Jumble-Man! Come on, let's get in.'

They all got in. The chair rose very slowly, and flew out of the door, taking care not to jerk or jolt the children at all. It flew so very slowly and carefully that Binky got quite impatient.

'Now you're being silly!' he said to the chair. 'Do fly properly. You're hardly moving.'

The chair flew faster. It flew very high and the children could hardly see the houses below them. They even flew above the clouds – and suddenly, to the children's great astonishment, they saw a big castle built on a cloud!

'I say! Look!' said Peter, in amazement. 'A castle on a cloud! Who lives there, Binky?'

'I don't know,' said Binky. 'I hope it's someone nice. I don't want to meet a giant this morning!'

The chair flew to the castle. There was a big front door standing open. The chair flew inside.

'Goodness!' said Mollie, in alarm. 'This isn't very polite. We ought to have knocked!'

The chair came to rest in a big kitchen. A small goblin, with pointed ears, green eyes and bony legs and arms, was sitting in a chair reading a paper. When the wishing-chair flew in with Binky, Mollie, and Peter in it, he jumped up in astonishment.

The children and Binky got out of their chair. 'Good morning,' said Binky. 'I'm so sorry to come in like this – but our chair didn't wait to knock.'

The goblin bowed politely. 'It doesn't matter at all!' he said. 'What a marvellous chair you have, and how pleased I am to see you! Pray sit down and let me give you some lemonade!'

They all sat down on stools. The goblin rushed to a cupboard and brought out a big jug of lemonade.

'It is so nice to see such pleasant visitors,' said the goblin, putting a glass of lemonade before each of them. 'And now, will you have biscuits?'

'Thank you,' said Mollie and Peter and Binky. They felt that it was kind of the goblin to welcome them – but they didn't like him at all. He seemed *much* too polite!

'Another glass of lemonade?' asked the goblin, taking Binky's empty glass. 'Oh do! It is a pleasure, I assure you, to have you here! Another biscuit, little girl? I make them myself, and only save them for *special* visitors.'

'But we aren't very special,' said Peter, thinking that the goblin was really silly to say such things.

'Oh yes, you are *very* special,' said the goblin, smiling politely at them all. '*So* good of you to come and see an ugly little goblin like me!'

'But we didn't *mean* to come and see you,' said Mollie truthfully. Binky frowned at her. He didn't want her to offend the goblin. He did not trust him at all. He wanted to get away as soon as he could.

'Well,' said Binky, finishing his biscuit, 'it is kind of you to have welcomed us like this. But now we must go.'

'Goodbye and thank you,' said the polite goblin. He shook hands with each of them and bowed very low. They turned to go to the wishing-chair.

And then they had a most *terrible* shock! The wishing-chair was not there! It was gone.

'I say! Where's the wishing-chair?' shouted Binky.
'Goblin, where's our chair?'

'Oh, pixie, how should *I* know?' said the goblin. 'Haven't
I been looking after you every minute? It must have flown
away when you were not looking.'

'Well, it's funny if it has,' said Binky. 'We should have
seen it, or at least felt the wind of its wings flapping. I don't
believe you, goblin. You have done something with our
chair – your servants have taken it away! Tell me quickly,
or I will punish you!'

'*Punish* me!' said the goblin. 'And how would you do
that, pray? You had better be careful, pixie – how are you
going to get away from my castle without a wishing-chair?
I live here by myself in the clouds!'

'Be careful, Binky,' said Peter. 'Don't make him angry. Goodness knows how we'd escape from here if he didn't help us!'

Mollie looked frightened. The little goblin smiled at her politely, and said, 'Don't be afraid, pretty little girl. I will treat you as an honoured guest for as long as you like to stay with me in my castle.'

'We don't want to stay with you at all,' said Binky. 'We want our wishing-chair! What have you DONE with it?'

But he could get no answer from the polite goblin. It was most tiresome. What in the world were they to do?

Binky suddenly lost his temper. He rushed at the goblin to catch him and shake him. The goblin looked scared. He turned to run and sped out of the big kitchen into the hall. Binky ran after him. Mollie and Peter looked at one another.

'Binky will get us all into trouble,' said Mollie. 'He really is a silly-billy. If he makes the goblin angry, he certainly won't help us to get away. I suppose that naughty wishing-chair flew away home.'

'I'm quite sure it didn't,' said Peter. 'I know I would have seen it moving.'

The goblin came running into the room followed by Binky. 'Catch him, catch him!' yelled Binky. Peter tried to – but the goblin was like an eel. He dodged this way, he dodged that way – and then a funny thing happened. Peter fell over something that wasn't there!

He crashed right into something and fell over, bang! And yet, when he looked, there was nothing at all to fall over! He felt very much astonished. He sat up and stared round. 'What did I fall over?' he said. Binky stopped chasing the goblin and ran to him. He put out his arms and felt round about in the air by Peter – and his hands closed on something hard – that couldn't be seen!

'Oh!' he yelled joyfully. 'It's the wishing-chair! That deceitful goblin made it invisible, so that we couldn't see it, even though it was really here! And he meant to help us home all right – and as soon as we had gone he meant to use our wishing-chair for himself, and we'd never know!'

'Then it hasn't flown away!' cried Mollie, running over and feeling it too. 'Oh goody, goody! We can get into it and go home even if we can't see what we're sitting on! Get up, Peter, and let's fly off before that nasty little polite goblin does any more spells!'

They all sat in the chair they couldn't see. 'Home, wishing-chair, home!' cried Binky. The invisible chair rose in the air and flew out of the door. The goblin ran to the door and bowed. 'So pleased to have seen you!' he called politely.

'Nasty little polite creature!' said Binky. 'My goodness – we nearly lost the chair, children! Now we've got to find a way of making it visible again. It's no fun having a chair and not knowing if it's really there or not! I don't like feeling I'm sitting on nothing! I like to *see* what I'm sitting on!'

They flew home. They got out of the chair and looked at one another.

'Well, we do have adventures!' said Peter, grinning.

CHAPTER 14
THE SPINNING HOUSE

It was most annoying not being able to see the wishing-chair. The children kept forgetting where it was and falling over it.

'Oh dear!' groaned Peter, picking himself up for the fourth time, 'I really can't bear this chair being invisible. I keep walking into it and bumping myself.'

'I'll tie a ribbon on it!' said Mollie. 'Then we shall see the ribbon in the air, and we'll know the chair is there!'

'That's a good idea,' said Binky. 'Girls always think of good ideas.'

'So do boys,' said Peter. 'I say! How queer that ribbon looks all by itself in the air! We can see it, but we can't see the chair it's tied on! People *would* stare if they came in here and saw it!'

It certainly did look funny. It stuck there in mid-air – and it did act as a warning to the children and Binky that they must be careful not to walk into the invisible chair. It saved them many a bump.

'I've been asking the fairies how we can get the chair made visible again,' said Binky the next day. 'They say there is a funny old witch who lives in a little spinning house in Jiffy Wood, who is very, very clever at making things invisible *or* visible! So if we fly there next time the chair grows wings, we may be able to have it put right.'

'But how shall we know when it grows its wings if we can't see them?' said Mollie.

'I never thought of that!' said Binky.

'I know!' said Peter. 'Let's tear up little bits of paper and put them round the legs of the chair on the floor! Then, when its wings grow, the bits will all fly about in the draught the wings make with their flapping – and we shall see them and know the chair is ready to go off adventuring again!'

The children tore up the bits of paper and put them on the floor near the legs of the chair.

'Really, it does look funny!' said Mollie. 'A ribbon balanced in mid-air – and bits of paper below, on the floor! Mother would think us very untidy if she came in.'

'Let's play tiddlywinks now,' said Peter. 'I'll get out the cup and the counters.'

Soon the three of them were playing tiddlywinks on the floor. Mollie flipped her counters into the cup very cleverly, and had just won, when Binky gave a shout:

'Look! Those bits of paper are fluttering into the air! The chair must have grown its wings!'

Mollie and Peter turned to look. Sure enough, the scraps of paper they had put on the floor were all dancing up and down as if a wind was blowing them. The children could feel a draught too, and knew that the wishing-chair had once again grown its red wings.

'That was a good idea of yours, Peter,' said Binky. 'Boys have good ideas as well as girls, I can see! Come on, let's get into the chair and see if it will fly to Jiffy Wood to the old witch's.'

They climbed on to the chair. It was really very strange climbing on to something they couldn't see, but could only feel. Binky sat on the back, as usual, and the children squeezed into the seat.

'Go to Jiffy Wood, to the little Spinning House,' Binky said to the chair. It rose up into the air, flew out of the door, and was up high before the children could say another word! They must have looked very queer, sitting in a chair that couldn't be seen!

It was raining. Mollie wished they had brought an umbrella. 'Tell the chair to fly above the clouds, Binky,' she said. 'It's the clouds that drop the rain on to us. If we fly beyond them, we shan't get wet because there won't be any rain.'

'Fly higher than the clouds, Chair,' said Binky. The chair rose higher and higher. It flew right through the misty grey clouds and came out above them. The sun was shining brightly! It made the other side of the clouds quite dazzling to look at!

'This is better,' said Mollie. 'The sun will dry our clothes.'

They flew on and on in the sunshine, above the great white clouds. Then they suddenly flew downwards again, and the children saw that they were over a thick wood.

'Jiffy Wood!' said Binky, peering down. 'We shall soon be there!'

Down they flew and down, and at last came to a little clearing. The chair flew down to it, and came to rest on some grass. A little way off was a most peculiar house. It had one leg, like a short pole, and it spun round and round and round on this leg! It did not go very fast, and the children could see that it had a door on one side and a window on each of the other three sides. It had one chimney which was smoking away merrily – but the smoke was green, a sign that a witch lived in the house.

'Well, here we are,' said Binky, getting out of the chair. 'I'd better carry the chair, I think. I don't like leaving it about here when we can't see it. We shouldn't know where it was if anyone came along and untied the ribbon.'

'Is the old witch a fierce sort of person?' asked Mollie.

'No, she's a good sort,' said Binky. 'She will do all she can to help us, I know. You needn't be afraid. She won't harm us. My grandmother knew her very well.'

'How are we going to get into the house?' asked Peter, looking at the strange house going round and round and round. 'It's like getting on a roundabout that's going! Our mother always says that's a dangerous thing to do.'

'Well, we'll try and get the witch to stop the house spinning round for a minute, so that we can hop in with the chair,' said Binky. 'Come on. I've got the chair.'

Off they went towards the queer little house. As it went round the smoke went round too, and made green rings. It was very peculiar.

'Witch Snippit, Witch Snippit!' called Binky. 'Stop your house and let us in!'

Someone opened a window and looked out. It was an old woman with a red shawl on and a pretty white cap. She had a hooky nose and a pair of large spectacles over her eyes. She seemed surprised to see them.

'Wait a minute!' she called. 'I'll stop the house. But you'll have to be very quick getting in at the door because it won't stop for long!'

The house slowed down – it went round more and more slowly – and at last it stopped. The door was facing the children, and the witch opened it and beckoned to them. Mollie shot inside, and so did Peter. Binky was trying to get in, with the chair too, when suddenly the house began to spin round fast again! Poor Binky fell out of the doorway with the chair!

Mollie and Peter really couldn't help laughing, he looked so funny! The witch stopped the house again, and then Peter helped Binky in quickly. They put the wishing-chair down and then turned to greet the witch.

'Good morning,' she said, with a nice smile. 'And what can I do for you?'

CHAPTER 15
WITCH SNIPPIT

The children and Binky looked at the smiling witch. They liked her very much. She had kind blue eyes, as bright as forget-me-nots. At first they felt rather giddy, for the house they were in spun round and round all the time – but they soon got used to it.

'We've brought our wishing-chair to you,' said Binky. 'We went to the cloud-goblin's castle the other day, and he made our chair invisible. It's such a nuisance to have a chair we can't see – so, as we knew you were clever at all kinds of visible and invisible spells, we thought we would bring it to you. Could you make our chair seeable, please?'

'Certainly,' said Witch Snippit. 'I have some very strong magic paint. If you use it, you will make your chair easily seen.'

She went to a cupboard. The children stared round the room.

It was a very strange room indeed. The clock on the mantelpiece had legs, and for every tick it gave, it walked a step along the mantelpiece.

When it got to the end it turned and walked back again. Then it suddenly disappeared!

'Ooh!' said Mollie, surprised. 'Your clock's gone, Witch Snippit!'

'Oh, don't take any notice of that,' said the witch. 'It's just showing off!'

The clock said 'Urrrrrrrr!' and came back again. Up and down it walked, and the children thought it was the strangest one they had ever seen.

Other things in the cottage were most peculiar too. There was a chair that had four legs and a back, but no seat. Mollie wondered if it really *had* got a seat that couldn't be seen. She went to sit down on it and found that it *had* got a seat, but it was quite invisible. There was a table too, that had a top but no legs.

On the dresser there were cups with no handles, and lids balanced in the air but no dishes below. Mollie put out her hand and felt the dishes, but she couldn't see them. She turned round to Witch Snippit.

'You *have* got a funny home,' she began – and then she stopped in surprise. Witch Snippit was all there except her middle! Oh dear, she did look so funny!

'Don't be worried,' she said to Mollie. 'I'm quite all right. My middle is really there, but it's vanished for a few minutes. You can't meddle about with visible and invisible magic without having things like this happen to you at times.'

As she spoke, her middle came back again, and, oh dear, her hands and feet went! Mollie began to laugh. 'Whatever will go next!' she said.

All of the witch disappeared then – and the children and Binky couldn't see her anywhere! They knew she was in the room, because they could hear her laughing.

'Don't look so surprised,' she said. 'You should never be astonished at anything that happens in a witch's house.'

'I say! The floor's gone!' said Peter, in alarm, looking down at his feet. 'Oooh! I feel as if I'm falling! Where's the floor?'

'Oh, it's there all the time,' said Witch Snippit, coming back in bits. 'It's only disappeared from sight. Don't worry, it's there!'

She put a tin of paint on the table. 'Would *you* like to paint your chair and get it right again?' she asked. 'It's quite easy. There are three brushes for you. It's good paint. It will make invisible things visible, or visible things *in*visible. I'm rather busy today, so if you'll do the job yourself, I'll be glad.'

'We'd love to!' said Binky. He took off the lid of the paint tin and picked up a brush. 'It's going to be funny painting something you can't see!' he said.

He felt for the legs of the chair and dipped his brush into the paint, which was a queer silvery colour and seemed as thin as smoke. He painted along one of the chair's invisible legs – and hey presto! it came into sight, as brown and solid as ever!

'I've got a leg back!' said Binky, in excitement, and waved his brush in the air. A drop of paint flew on to Peter's nose.

'Don't,' said Peter. Mollie stared at him in horror. His nose had disappeared!

'Peter, your nose has gone!' she said. 'A drop of the paint went on to it! Oh, whatever shall we do?'

'Get it back again, of course,' said Binky. 'Didn't you hear Witch Snippit say that this paint acted either way? It makes things seen that can't be seen, and it makes things that are seeable *un*seeable! Come here, Peter – I'll paint where your nose should be, and it'll come back again!'

He dabbed some paint where he thought Peter's nose should be – and sure enough, it *did* come back again! Mollie was so glad. Peter looked horrid without a nose.

'I'll teach you to make my nose disappear!' said Peter to Binky. He dipped his brush in the paint and dabbed at Binky's pointed ears. They vanished in a trice.

'Don't!' said Binky crossly. He threw some paint at Peter's feet and they disappeared at once!

'Oh!' said Peter, surprised. 'I don't like having no feet. I shall paint them back! There they are! Stop it, Binky. I don't like this game. It would be awful if something *didn't* come back!'

Binky was naughty. He dipped his brush in the magic paint, and ran it round Mollie's neck. How queer she looked with a head and a body but no neck! Peter couldn't bear it. He painted her neck in again at once, and frowned at Binky.

'If you're not careful I'll paint you from top to toe and then take away the tin of paint!' he said.

'Now listen to me,' suddenly said Witch Snippit's voice above them. 'I didn't give you that paint to waste. If you are not careful there will not be enough to finish painting your wishing-chair, and then you will find there is a bit still left invisible, that you cannot see. So be sensible.'

Binky and Peter went red. They began to paint the chair busily, and Mollie joined them. The clock on the mantelpiece was so interested in what they were doing that it walked right off the mantelpiece and fell into the coal scuttle.

'It can stay there,' said the witch. 'It is much too curious – always poking its nose where it isn't wanted.'

'Urrrrrrrrr!' said the clock, and disappeared. Mollie was glad her clock at home didn't behave like that.

In an hour's time the wishing-chair was itself again, and all the paint in the tin was finished. There it stood before them, their same old wishing-chair. It had been very strange to see it gradually becoming visible to their eyes.

'There's a bit at the back here that can't be seen,' said Mollie, pointing to a bit that hadn't come back again. But there was no paint to finish that bit, and the children didn't like to ask for any more. So that tiny piece of the chair had

to remain invisible. It looked like a hole!

'Thank you very much, Witch Snippit,' said Binky politely. 'We've finished now, and had better be getting home. Could you stop your house spinning and let us go out?'

'Very well,' said Witch Snippit. She called out a magic word and the spinning house slowed down. 'Goodbye,' she said to Binky and the children. 'Come and see me again another time. Hurry, now, or the house will start spinning again!'

The three squeezed into the wishing-chair. The house stopped and the witch opened the door.

'Home, wishing-chair!' shouted Binky – and the chair flew straight out of the door and up into the air.

'Goodbye, goodbye!' called Mollie and Peter, looking down at the house, which was already spinning fast again.

'I say, that was a pretty good adventure, wasn't it!'

'I wish we'd got some of that magic paint with us,' said Binky. 'We could have some fun with it!'

'I'm glad we haven't!' said Mollie. 'I don't know *what* mischief you'd get into, Binky!'

CHAPTER 16

THE SILLY BOY

The children were cross because Mother had said that the painters were to paint the walls of the playroom and mend a window – and this meant that they couldn't play there for some time.

Their playroom was built right at the bottom of the garden, and it was quite safe for their friend, Binky, the pixie, to live there, for no one ever went to the garden playroom except themselves. But now the painters would be there for a week. How tiresome!

'It's a good thing it's summer-time, Binky, so that you can live in the garden for a bit,' said Mollie.

'Oh, don't worry about *me*,' said Binky. 'I've a nice cosy place in the hollow of an oak tree. It's the chair I'm thinking about. Where shall we keep that? We can't have it flying about whilst the painters are there.'

'We'd better put it in the boxroom, indoors,' said Peter. 'That room's just been repainted so I don't expect Mother or anyone will think it must be turned out just yet. It will be safe there.'

So, when no one was looking, Peter and Mollie carried the wishing-chair up to the boxroom and stood it safely in a corner. They shut the window up tightly, so that it couldn't fly out if its wings grew suddenly.

They couldn't have Binky to play with them in the house, because he didn't want anyone to know about him. So they asked Thomas, the little boy over the road, to come and play soldiers, on a rainy afternoon.

They didn't like him very much, but he was better than nobody.

Thomas came. He soon got tired of playing soldiers. He began turning head-over-heels down the nursery floor. He could do it very well.

'I can make awful faces too,' he said to Mollie and Peter – and he began to pull such dreadful faces that the two children gazed at him in surprise and horror.

'Our mother says that if you pull faces and the wind happens to change you may get stuck like that,' said Mollie. 'Do stop it, Thomas.'

But Thomas wouldn't. He wrinkled up his nose and his forehead and blew out his cheeks – and do you know, the wind changed that very minute! And poor Thomas couldn't get his face right again! He tried and he tried, but he couldn't. It was dreadful! Whatever was he to do?

'Oh, Thomas, the wind changed – I saw the weather-cock swing round that very moment!' cried Mollie. 'I did warn you! I do think you're silly.'

'He can't go home like that,' said Peter. 'Let's wash his face in hot water – then perhaps it will go right again.'

So they washed Thomas's face well – but it was as bad as ever when they had finished! Screwed-up nose and forehead and blown-out cheeks ... oh dear!

'Do you suppose Binky would know what to do?' said Peter at last.

'Who's Binky?' asked Thomas.

'Never you mind,' said Mollie. 'Peter, go and find Binky and see what he says. I'll stay here with Thomas. He mustn't go out of the nursery, because if he meets Mother or Jane, they will think he's making faces at them and will be ever so cross.

Peter ran downstairs. He went into the garden and whistled a little tune that Binky had taught him. He had to whistle this whenever he wanted the pixie.

Binky whistled back. Peter saw him under a big hawthorn bush, mending a hole in his coat.

'What's up?' asked Binky, sewing away.

'We've got a boy in our nursery who's been making dreadful faces,' explained Peter. 'And the wind changed just as he was making a specially horrible one – and now he can't get his face right again. So Mollie sent me to ask you if you could do anything to help.''

'A boy as silly as that doesn't deserve help,' said Binky, breaking off his cotton and threading his needle again. 'You go and tell him so.'

'Oh no, Binky, we really *must* help him,' said Peter. 'His mother may think *we* made his face like that, and we'll get into trouble. You don't want us to be sent to bed for a week, do you?'

'No, I don't,' said Binky, putting on his coat. 'I'll help *you* because you're my friends. There's only one thing to be done for a person who's been making faces when the wind changed.'

'What's that?' asked Peter.

'You've got to get a bit of the wind that blew just then, and puff it into his face,' said Binky. 'Then he'll be all right – but it's dreadfully difficult to get a bit of the same wind.'

'How can we?' asked Peter, in dismay.

'We'd better go in the wishing-chair to the Windy Wizard,' said Binky. 'He knows all the ins and outs of every wind that blows. I've seen the old wishing-chair looking out of the window this afternoon, trying to get out, so I'm sure it's grown its wings again. Go and see, and if it has, tell Mollie, and we'll go and get help from the old wizard.'

'Oh, thank you, Binky,' said Peter, and he ran indoors. He whispered to Mollie all that Binky had said.

'I think the chair *must* have grown its wings,' Mollie

said, 'because there have been such queer sounds going on in the boxroom this afternoon – you know, knockings and bumping. I expect it's the chair trying to get out.'

'I'll go and see,' said Peter. He ran up the top-most flight of stairs and opened the boxroom door. The wishing-chair was standing by it, ready to fly out – but Peter caught hold of it just as it was slipping out of the door.

'Now just wait a minute,' he said. But the chair wouldn't! It forced its way past Peter and the little boy jumped into it. 'Go to Binky!' he called hoping that the chair wouldn't meet anyone on the way.

The chair flew down the stairs and out into the garden. It went to where Binky was standing by the hawthorn bush. It was flapping its red wings madly and Binky jumped into it at once.

'To the Windy Wizard's!' he shouted. 'I say, Peter, isn't it in a hurry! It must have got tired of being shut up in the boxroom!'

Mollie was looking out of the window. She had heard the chair flying downstairs. She saw it up in the air, carrying Peter and Binky, and she wished she were in it too!

'Someone's got to stay with Thomas, though,' she thought to herself. 'He'd only run home or go and find our mother or something, if we left him quite alone. What an ugly face he has now! I do hope Peter and Binky find something to put it right!'

CHAPTER 17

THE WINDY WIZARD

The wishing-chair rose high into the air, carrying Peter and Binky. It had stopped raining and was a hot sunny day and the wind the chair made rushing through the air was very pleasant. Peter wished Mollie was with them. It was much more fun to go on adventures all together.

Presently the chair came into a very windy sky. Goodness, how the wind blew! It blew the white clouds to rags. It blew Peter's hair nearly off his head! It blew the chair's wings so that it could hardly flap them.

'The Windy Wizard lives somewhere about here,' said Binky, looking down. 'Look! Do you see that hill over there, golden with buttercups? There's a house there. It's the Windy Wizard's, I'm sure, because it's rocking about in all directions as if the wind lived inside it!'

Down flew the wishing-chair. It came to rest outside the cottage, which was certainly rocking about in a most alarming manner. Peter and Binky jumped off and ran to the cottage door. They knocked.

'Come in!' cried a voice. They opened the door and went in. Oooh! The wind rushed out at them and nearly blew them off their feet!

'Goodday!' said the Windy Wizard. He was a most

peculiar-looking person, for he had long hair and a very long beard and a cloak that swept to the ground, but, as the wind blew his hair and beard and cloak up and down and round and about all the time, it was very difficult to see what he was really like!

'Good day,' said Peter and Binky, staring at the wizard. He hadn't a very comfortable house to live in, Peter thought, because there were draughts everywhere, round his legs, down his neck, behind his knees! And all the cottage was full of a whispering, sighing sound as if a wind was talking to itself all the time.

'Have you come to buy a little wind?' asked the wizard.

'No,' said Binky. 'I've come about a boy who made faces when the wind changed – and he can't get right again. So we thought perhaps you could help us. I know that if we could get a little of the wind that blew at that time, and puff it into his face, he'll be all right – but how can we get the wind?'

'What a foolish boy!' said the Windy Wizard, his cloak blowing out and hiding him completely. 'What time did this happen?'

'At half-past three this afternoon,' said Peter. 'I heard the nursery clock strike.'

'It's difficult, very difficult,' said the wizard, smoothing down his cloak. 'You see, the wind blows and is gone in a trice! Now let me think for a moment – who is likely to have kept a little of that wind?'

'What about the birds that were flying in the air at that moment?' asked Binky. 'They may have some in their feathers, you know.'

'Yes, so they may,' said the wizard. He took a feather from a jar that was full of them, and flung it out of the door.

'Come, birds, and bring
The breeze from your wing!'

he chanted.

Peter and Binky looked out of the door, hoping that dozens of birds would come – but only one appeared, and that was a blackbird.

'Only one bird was flying in the air with the wind at that moment,' said the wizard. 'Come, blackbird, shake your feathers. I want the wind from them!'

The blackbird shook his glossy feathers out and the wizard held a green paper bag under them to catch the wind in them. The bag blew up a little, like a balloon.

'Not enough wind here to change your friend's face back again!' said the wizard, looking at it. 'I wonder if there were any kites using the wind at that moment!'

He went to a cupboard and took the tail of a kite out of it. He threw it up into the air just outside the door.

'Come, kites, and bring
The breeze from your wing!'

he called.

Peter and Binky watched eagerly – and to their delight saw two kites sailing down from the sky. One was a green one and one was a red. They fell at the wizard's feet.

He shook each one to get the wind into his green bag. It blew up just a little more.

'Still not enough,' said the wizard. 'I'll get the little ships along. There will surely be enough then!'

He ran to the mantelpiece and took a tiny sailor doll from it. He threw it up into the air and it disappeared.

'Come, ships, and bring
The breeze from your wing!'

sang the old wizard, his hair and beard streaming out like smoke.

Then, sailing up a tinkling stream that ran down the

hillside came six little toy sailing ships, their sails full of the wind. They sailed right up to the wizard's front door, for the stream suddenly seemed to run there – and quickly and neatly the old wizard seized each ship, shook its sails into the green paper bag, and then popped it back on the stream. Away sailed the ships again and Peter and Binky saw them no more.

The paper bag was quite fat and full now.

'That's about enough, I think,' said the wizard. 'Now I'll put the wind into a pair of bellows for you!'

He took a small pair of bellows from his fireside and put the tip of them into the green paper bag. He opened the bellows and they sucked in all the air from the bag. The wizard handed them to Peter and Binky.

'Now don't puff with these bellows until you reach your friend,' he said. 'Then use them hard and puff all the air into his face! It will come right again in a twink!'

'Thank you so much for your help,' said Binky gratefully. He and Peter ran to the wishing-chair again and climbed into it, holding the bellows carefully. The chair rose up into the air as Binky cried, 'Home, Chair, home!'

In a few minutes it was flying in at the boxroom window, for Mollie had run up and opened it, ready for the chair when it came back again. Peter and Binky shut the window after them, ran down to the nursery and burst in at the door.

Thomas was still there, his face screwed up and his cheeks blown out!

'I'm so glad you're back!' said Mollie. 'It's horrid being

here with Thomas. His face is so nasty to look at, it makes me feel I'm in a dream! Have you got something to make it right?'

'Yes,' said Binky, showing her the bellows. 'The Windy Wizard has filled these bellows full of the wind that blew when Thomas made that face. If we puff it at him, his face will be all right again!'

'Go on then, puff!' said Mollie. So Binky lifted up the bellows and puffed them right into Thomas's face – phoooooof! Thomas gasped and spluttered. He shut his eyes and coughed – and when he opened them, his face had gone right again! His nose and forehead were no longer screwed up, and his cheeks were quite flat, not a bit blown up!

'You're right again now, Thomas,' said Binky. 'But let it be a lesson to you not to be silly any more.'

'I'll never pull faces again,' said Thomas, who had really

had a dreadful fright. 'But who are you? Are you a fairy?'

'Never mind who I am, and don't say a word about me or what has happened this afternoon!' said Binky, and Thomas promised. He ran home feeling puzzled, but very happy to think that he had got his face its right shape again.

'Well, that was an exciting sort of adventure, Mollie!' said Peter, and he told her all about it. 'The Windy Wizard was *so* nice. I say – what about giving him back his bellows?'

'I'll manage that,' said Binky, taking them. 'I must go now or someone will come into the nursery and see me! Goodbye till next time!'

CHAPTER 18

MR TWISTY

One day, when the two children and Binky were in their playroom at the bottom of the garden, reading quietly, a knock sounded at the door.

They looked up. A small man stood there, with his straw hat in his hand and a sly look on his face.

'Have you anything old to sell?' he asked. 'I buy old clothes, furniture, carpets – anything you like. I'll give you a good price for it too.'

'No, thank you,' said Mollie. 'We couldn't sell anything unless our mother said so.'

'What about that old chair there?' said the man, pointing to the wishing-chair. 'It can't be wanted or you wouldn't have it in your playroom. I like the look of that. I'll give you a good price for that.'

'Certainly not!' said Peter. 'Please go away, or I'll call the gardener.'

The little man put on his straw hat, grinned at them all, and went. Binky looked uncomfortable. 'I don't like the look of him,' he said to the children. 'He may make trouble for us. I think I'll hop out into the garden today. I don't like people seeing me here.'

So he hopped out and went to play with the fairy folk

there – and a good thing he did too – for in about ten minutes Mother came down the garden followed by the little man in the straw hat.

'Are you there, Peter and Mollie?' she said. 'Oh, this man, Mr Twisty, says he will buy anything old – and he saw an old chair here he would like to buy. I couldn't remember it – which is it?'

Poor Mollie and Peter! They had kept their wishing-chair such a secret – and now the secret was out! They really didn't know what to say.

Mother saw the chair and looked puzzled. 'I don't remember that chair at all,' she said.

'I'll give you two pounds for it,' said Mr Twisty. ''Tisn't worth it – but I'll take it for that.'

'That seems a lot of money for a playroom chair,' said Mother. 'Well, fetch it tonight, and you can have it.'

'Oh, Mother, Mother!' shrieked the two children in despair. 'You don't understand. It's our own, very own chair. We love it. It's a very precious sort of chair.'

'Whatever do you mean?' said Mother, in surprise. 'It doesn't look at all precious to me.'

Well, Mollie and Peter knew quite well that they couldn't say it was a wishing-chair and grew wings. It would be taken away from them at once, then, and put into a museum or something. Whatever were they to do?

'Two pounds for that dirty old chair,' said Mr Twisty, looking slyly at Mother.

'Very well,' said Mother.

'I'll send for it tonight,' said Mr Twisty, and he bowed and went off up the garden path.

'Don't look so upset, silly-billies!' said Mother. 'I'll buy you a nice comfy wicker-chair instead.'

Mollie and Peter said nothing. Mollie burst into tears as soon as Mother had gone. 'It's too bad!' she sobbed. 'It's our own wishing-chair – and that horrible Mr Twisty is buying it for two pounds.'

Binky came in, and they told him what had happened. He grinned at them, and put his arm round Mollie. 'Don't cry,' he said. 'I've got a good plan.'

'What?' asked Mollie.

'I can get Mr Knobbles, the pixie carpenter who lives out in the field over there, to make me a chair almost exactly like the wishing-chair!' said Binky. 'We'll let Mr Twisty have that one – not ours! He won't know the difference.

He doesn't know ours is a wishing-chair – he just thinks it's an old and valuable chair. Well, he can buy one just like it – without the magic in it!'

'Ooh!' said Mollie and Peter, pleased. 'Can you really get one made in time?'

'I think so,' said Binky. 'Come along with me and see.'

So they squeezed under the hedge at the bottom of the garden and crossed the field beyond to where a big oak tree stood. Binky pulled a root aside, that stuck out above the ground, and under it was a trap-door!

'You simply *never* know where the little folk live!' said Mollie excitedly.

Binky rapped on the door. It flew up and a bald-headed pixie with enormous ears popped his head out. Binky explained what he wanted and the pixie invited them into his workshop underground. It was a dear little place, scattered with small tables, chairs and stools that the carpenter had been making.

'Do you think you could make us the chair in time?' asked Mollie eagerly.

'Well, if I could get a quick-spell, I could,' said the pixie. 'A quick-spell makes you work three times as fast as usual, you know. But they are so expensive.'

'Oh,' said Mollie and Peter, in dismay. 'Well, we've hardly any money.'

'Wait!' said Binky, grinning at them in his wicked way. 'Remember that Mr Twisty is paying two pounds for the chair! Can you make the chair and buy the quick-spell for two pounds, Mr Knobbles?'

Mr Knobbles worked out a sum on a bit of paper and

said he just could. He came back to the playroom with the children and saw their own chair. He nodded his head and said he could easily make one just the same. The children were so pleased. They hugged Binky and said he was the cleverest person they had ever known. He always knew just how to get them out of any difficulty.

'Now, we'd better hide our own chair,' said Binky. 'Where shall we put it?'

'In the gardener's shed!' said Mollie. 'Gardener will be gone at five. We'll put it there, then.'

So they did, and covered it up with sacks. Just as they came back from the shed, they met Mr Knobbles carrying on his back a new chair, just *exactly* like their old one! It was marvellous!

'The quick-spell worked quickly!' he said. 'Here's the chair. You can bring me the money any time.'

The children thanked him and put the chair in their playroom. Then they waited for Mr Twisty.

He turned up for it at half-past six, his straw hat in his hand, and the usual wide smile on his sly face. 'Ah, there's the chair!' he said. 'Here's the money! Thank you very much!'

He took the chair on his back, paid over the money and went, whistling a tune.

'Well, he's got a marvellous pixie-chair for his money,' said Binky, 'but he hasn't got a wishing-chair! He can sell that chair for twenty pounds, I should think – for Mr Knobbles has made it beautifully – hasn't used a single nail – stuck everything with magic glue!'

'And *we've* got our own dear chair still!' cried the two children, and sat down in it for joy.

Just then Mother popped her head in – and saw the chair! Binky only *just* had time to hide himself behind the sofa!

'Why!' she said. 'The chair isn't sold after all! I'm quite glad, because it really is a pretty chair. I can't imagine how I came to let you have it in your playroom. I think I will have it in the house. Bring it up with you tonight, Peter.'

Mother went away again. Binky popped out from his hiding place and looked at the others in dismay.

'I say!' he said. 'That's bad news. You'll have to do as you're told, Peter. Take the chair up to the house with you when you go tonight – and we'll try and think of some way out of this new fix. Oh dear! Why can't we have our own chair!'

So Peter took it up to the house with him – and Mother put it into the study. Suppose it grew wings there! Whatever would happen?

CHAPTER 19

TWO BAD CHILDREN

Mollie and Peter were very upset. Mother had got their wishing-chair in the study – and if it grew its wings there the grown-ups might see them – and then their great secret would be known. Whatever could be done about it?

Binky had no ideas at all. He simply didn't know how to get the chair back into the playroom. If they just took it back, Mother would notice and would have it brought to the house again.

Peter and Mollie thought very hard how to get the chair for their own again – and at last Mollie had an idea. She and Peter ran down to the playroom to tell Binky.

'This is my idea,' said Mollie. 'It's a very naughty one and we shall get into trouble – but I don't see how we can help it. After all, it *is* our chair!'

'Go on, tell us your plan,' said Peter.

'It's this,' said Mollie. 'Let's spill things over the chair – and tear the seat or something – and scratch the legs! Then, when Mother sees how dirty and scratched and torn it is, she won't think it is good enough for the study – and perhaps we can have it back again!'

'I say! That's a really good idea!' said Peter and Binky together.

'But we *shall* get into trouble!' said Peter. 'You know how Mother hates us to mess things – that's why we have this playroom at the bottom of the garden – so that we can do as we like and not spoil things in the dining-room or drawing-room or study up at the house.'

'Well, even if we do get into trouble it will be worth it if we can get back our chair,' said Mollie. 'I don't mind being punished if we can only go for some more adventures.'

'All right,' said Peter. 'I don't either. What shall we do first?'

'We'll spill some ink across the seat,' said Mollie.

'Come on, then,' said Peter. So they shouted goodbye to Binky, who wished them good luck, and ran up to the house. They went into the study. The wishing-chair stood there, looking very good and proper. Mother had put a fine new cushion into it. Mollie took it out. She didn't want to spoil anything that belonged to Mother.

Peter got the ink bottle, and the two children emptied ink across the seat of the chair. Then they went to tell Mother.

She *was* cross! 'How very, very careless of you!' she scolded. 'You shall not go out to tea today, Peter and Mollie. I am very much annoyed with you. It's a good thing the ink didn't get on to my new cushion.'

Mollie and Peter said nothing. They did not go out to tea that day, and they were sad about it – but they kept thinking that perhaps they might get their wishing-chair back – so they did not get too unhappy.

The next day Peter sat in the wishing-chair and kicked his boots against the legs as hard as he could, so that they were scratched and dented. Mother heard him kicking and put her head into the study to see what was going on there.

'Peter!' she cried. 'Why aren't you out in the garden on this fine day – and do stop kicking your feet against that chair! Oh, you bad boy, see what you have done!'

She ran over to the chair and looked at the legs. They *were* scratched!

'This is very naughty, Peter,' said Mother. 'Yesterday you and Mollie spilt ink on this chair – and now you have kicked it like this. You will go to bed for the rest of the day!'

Poor Peter! He went very red, but he marched upstairs without a word. It was horrid to have to be so careless with a chair, especially one he loved so much – but still, somehow or other he *had* to get it back to the playroom! Suppose it grew its wings when Mother was sitting in it and flew away with her. Whatever would she do? She would be so frightened!

Mollie was sorry that Peter had been sent to bed. She crept into his room and gave him a piece of chocolate to eat.

'I'm going to slit the seat now,' she whispered. 'I expect I'll be sent to bed too – but surely after that Mother will say the chair isn't good enough for the study and we'll have it back again!'

So Mollie went downstairs, and took her work-basket into the study. She got out her scissors and began to cut out some dolls' clothes – and then, oh dear, she ran her scissors into the seat of the chair and made a big cut there!

Mother came in after a while – and she saw the slit at once. She stared in horror.

'Mollie! Did you do that?'

'I'm afraid I did, Mother,' said Mollie.

'Then you are as bad as Peter,' said Mother crossly. 'Go to bed too. This chair is simply dreadful now – inky, torn, and scratched! It will have to go back to the playroom. I can't have it in the study. You are two bad children, and I am ashamed of you both.'

It was dreadful to have Mother so cross. Mollie cried when she got into bed – but she was comforted when she thought that the wishing-chair was really going back to the playroom. She and Peter had to stay in bed all day, and they were very tired of it. But when the next day came, they carried the chair back to their playroom and called Binky.

'We've got the chair, Binky!' they cried. 'Hurrah! But we did get into trouble. We both went to bed for the day, and Mother was dreadfully cross. We shall have to be extra nice to her now to make up – because we didn't really mean to vex her. Only we *had* to get the chair back somehow!'

'Good for you!' said Binky, pleased. He looked at the chair and grinned.

'My word!' he said. 'You did do some damage to it, didn't you! What a mess it's in! Mollie, you'd better get your needle and cotton and mend the seat – and Peter and I had better polish up the legs a bit and try and hide the scratches!'

So that morning the children and Binky worked hard at the chair and by dinner-time it really looked very much better. Mollie put back into it the cushion they always had there, and then clapped her hands for joy.

'Dear old wishing-chair!' she said. 'It's nice to have you again! Mr Twisty nearly got you – and Mother nearly had you too – but now we've got you back again at last!'

'And *I'm* longing for another adventure!' said Peter. 'I wish it would grow its wings again!'

'It soon will!' said Binky. 'I expect it wants another adventure as much as we do!'

CHAPTER 20

THE HORRID QUARREL

One morning Mollie, Peter and Binky were playing in the playroom at the bottom of the garden. It had been raining all morning, which was horrid in the summer-time. The children and the pixie were very tired of staying indoors.

They had played ludo and snap and draughts and snakes and ladders and dominoes. Now there didn't seem any other game to play, and they were getting cross and bored.

'Cheer up, Peter!' said Mollie, looking at Peter's cross face. 'You look like a monkey that's lost its tail.'

'And you look like a giraffe with a sore throat,' said Peter rudely.

'Don't be horrid!' said Mollie.

'Well, don't you, then,' said Peter.

'I'm not,' said Mollie.

'You are,' said Peter.

'Now be quiet, you two,' said Binky. 'I don't like to hear you quarrelling. You only get silly.'

'Don't interfere,' said Peter crossly. 'You talk too much, Binky.'

'Yes, remember we've been given two ears but only one mouth – so you should talk only half as much as you hear,' said Mollie.

'Same to you,' said Binky. 'All girls talk too much.'

'They *don't*!' said Mollie. 'How horrid of you to say that, Binky.'

'You're horrid this morning too,' said Binky. 'You're both horrid.'

'Well, if you think that, just go away and play somewhere else,' said Mollie at once. '*We* don't want you!'

'All right then, I will!' said Binky, offended – and to the children's dismay he got up and walked out of the playroom!

'There! Now see what you've done!' said Peter, getting up. 'Sent Binky away! Suppose he doesn't come back!'

He ran to the door and called, 'Binky! Hie, Binky! Come back a minute!'

But there was no answer. Binky had gone. There was no sign of him anywhere.

'I do think you are horrid and silly,' said Peter to Mollie. 'Fancy sending Binky away like that!'

'I didn't mean to,' said Mollie, almost in tears. 'He was being horrid, so I was too. We were all being horrid.'

'*I* wasn't,' said Peter.

'Yes, you were,' said Mollie.

'No, I wasn't,' said Peter.

'Yes, you were,' said Mollie. 'I shall smack you in a minute.'

'Now, now!' said a voice, and Mother looked in at the door. 'You are silly to quarrel like that! Uncle Jack is here and wants to know if you would like to go with him to the farm. They have some puppies there, and he wants to choose one for himself. Would you like to go and help him?'

'Oh yes!' cried Peter and Mollie. 'We'll put on our macs and rubber boots and go with him!'

So off they ran, forgetting all about their quarrel – and all about Binky too! They went to the farm with Uncle Jack and chose a lovely black puppy with him. Then back home they went, chattering and laughing, forgetting all about how horrid they had been, and enjoying their lovely walk.

It was dinner-time when they got home. They had dinner and ran down to the playroom afterwards, meaning to ask Binky to play with them in the field outside the garden.

But Binky wasn't in the playroom. Peter and Mollie looked at one another and went red.

'Do you suppose he has *really* gone?' said Mollie, feeling upset.

'I don't know,' said Peter. 'I'll whistle for him outside and see if he comes trotting out of the bushes!'

So Peter went to the door and whistled the little pixie tune that Binky had taught him. But no Binky came trotting up. It was really horrid.

'Suppose he never, never comes again!' said Mollie, crying. 'Oh, I do, do wish I'd never said that to him – telling him to go away. I didn't really mean it.'

'I shan't like going on adventures in the wishing-chair unless Binky is with us,' said Peter. 'It isn't any fun without him.'

'Peter, do you suppose he will *never* come and see us again?' asked Mollie.

'I shouldn't be surprised,' said Peter. 'Pixies are funny, you know – not quite like ordinary people.'

The two children would have been very unhappy indeed if something hadn't suddenly happened to take their minds away from their disappointment. The wishing-chair suddenly grew its wings again!

'Look!' said Mollie excitedly. 'The chair is ready to fly off again. Shall we go, Peter?'

'I don't feel as if I want to, now Binky's not here,' said Peter gloomily.

'But, Peter, I've such a good idea!' said Mollie, running to him. 'Listen! Let's get in the wishing-chair and tell it to go to Binky's home, wherever it is. I expect he's gone back there, don't you? Then we can say we're sorry and ask him to come back again.'

'That's a fine idea,' said Peter, at once. 'Come on, Mollie. Get in! We'll go at once.'

So the two children squeezed into the wishing-chair. It had grown its four red wings round its legs and was lazily flapping them to and fro, longing to be off into the air once more.

'Go to Binky's home,' commanded Peter. The chair rose up into the air, flew out of the door and rose high above the trees. It was fun to fly again. The two children looked down on the gardens and fields, and wished Binky were with them, sitting in his usual place on the top of the chair!

'I wonder where Binky's home *is*,' said Peter. 'He has never told us.'

'We shall soon see,' said Mollie.

The chair flew on and on, just below the clouds. Soon it came to the towers and spires of Fairyland. Then it suddenly flew downwards to a little village of quaint

crooked houses, all of them small, and all of them with bright flowery gardens. The chair flew down into one of the gardens and rested there. The children jumped off at once.

They went to the little red door of the house and knocked.

'Won't Binky be surprised to see us!' said Mollie.

The door opened. An old pixie woman, with a very sweet face and bright eyes, looked out at them.

'Oh!' said Mollie, in disappointment. 'We thought this was Binky's home.'

'So it is when he is at home!' said the pixie woman. 'I'm his mother. Come in, please.'

They went into a neat and spotless little kitchen. Binky's mother set ginger buns and lemonade in front of them.

'Thank you,' said Peter. 'Do you know where Binky is?'

'He came and asked me to make up his bed for tonight,' said the pixie woman. 'He said he had quarrelled with you, and wanted to come and live at home again.'

The children went red. 'I didn't mean what I said,' said Mollie, in a little voice.

'I expect Binky was to blame too,' said his mother. 'He went out to buy himself a new handkerchief – and though I've been waiting and waiting for him he hasn't come back – so I wondered if he had gone back to you again.'

'No, he didn't come back,' said Peter. 'I wonder what's happened to him. We'll stay a little while, if you don't mind, and see if he comes back.'

Binky didn't come back – but in a short while a round,

fat pixie came running up the path and into the kitchen, puffing and panting.

'Oh, Mrs Twinkle!' he cried, when he saw Binky's mother. 'A dreadful thing has happened to Binky!'

'What!' cried everyone in alarm.

'He had bought himself a nice new red handkerchief and was walking down the lane home again when a big yellow bird swooped down from the air, caught hold of Binky by the belt, and flew off with him!' cried the pixie.

'Oh my, oh my!' wept Mrs Twinkle. 'I know that bird. It belongs to the enchanter Clip-clap. He always sends that bird of his out when he wants to capture someone to help him. Poor Binky!'

'Don't cry!' said Peter, putting his arms round the old woman. 'We'll go and look for Binky. The magic chair we have will take us. We will try to bring him back safely. It's a very good thing we came to look for him! Come on, Mollie – get into the wishing-chair and we'll tell it to go to wherever Binky is!'

In they both got. Peter told the chair to go to Binky, and it rose into the air.

'Another adventure!' said Mollie. 'I do hope it turns out all right!'

CHAPTER 21
THE ENCHANTER CLIP-CLAP

The wishing-chair rose high up and flew steadily towards the west. It had a long way to go so it flew faster than usual, and all its four wings flapped swiftly.

'I wonder where the enchanter lives,' said Mollie. 'I hope he won't capture us too!'

'Well, all this would never have happened if we hadn't quarrelled with Binky,' said Peter. 'He wouldn't have gone back home then – and wouldn't have gone out to buy a new handkerchief – and wouldn't have been captured by the yellow bird that swooped down on him and took him away!'

'I shall never quarrel again,' said Mollie. It made her very sad when she remembered the unkind things she had said that morning.

The chair flew over a wood. Mollie leaned over the arm of the chair and looked down.

'Look, Peter,' she said. 'What is that funny thing sticking out of the wood?'

Peter looked. 'It's a very, very high stone tower,' he said. 'Isn't it strange? It's just a tower by itself. It doesn't seem to be part of a castle or anything. I say! The chair is flying down to it! Do you suppose that is where the enchanter lives?'

'It must be,' said Mollie. The children looked eagerly downwards to see what sort of tower this was. It certainly was very queer. It had a pointed roof but no chimneys at all. The chair circled all round it as it flew downwards, trying to find a window. But there was not a single window to be seen!

'This really is a very magic sort of tower!' said Mollie. 'Not a window anywhere! Well, there must be a door at the bottom to get in by.'

The chair flew to the ground and stayed there. The children jumped off. They went to the tower and looked for a door. There was not one to be seen!

The tower was quite round, and very tall indeed, higher than the highest tree – but it had no doors and no windows, so it seemed quite impossible to get into it. Mollie and Peter walked round and round it a great many times, but no matter how they looked, they could see no way to get in.

'Do you suppose Binky is in there,' said Mollie at last.

'Sure to be,' said Peter gloomily. 'We told the chair to take us to where Binky was, you know.'

'Well, what are we going to do?' asked Mollie. 'Shall we call for Binky loudly?'

'No,' said Peter at once. 'If you do that the enchanter will know we are here and may capture us too. Don't do anything like that, Mollie.'

'Well, how else are we to tell Binky we are here?' said Mollie. 'We must *do* something, Peter. It's no good standing here looking for doors and windows that aren't there.'

'Sh!' said Peter suddenly, and he pulled Mollie behind a tree. He had heard a noise.

Mollie caught hold of the wishing-chair and pulled that behind the tree too – and only just in time!

There came a loud noise, like the clip-clapping of thunder. A great door appeared in the round tower, half as high as the tower itself. It opened – and out came the enchanter Clip-clap! He was very tall and thin, and he had a long beard that reached the ground. He wore it in a plait and it looked very queer.

'See you finish that spell properly!' he called to someone in the tower. Then there came another loud clapping noise, just like a roll and crash of thunder, and the door in the tower closed – and vanished! The enchanter strode away through the wood, his head almost as high as the trees!

'Goodness!' said Mollie. 'We only just got behind this tree in time. It's impossible to get into that tower, Peter. We should never know how to make that door appear.'

'What *are* we to do!' sighed Peter. 'I hate to think of poor old Binky a prisoner in there – and all because we quarrelled with him too.'

'Let's hide the chair under a bush and see if we can find anyone living near here,' said Mollie. 'We might find someone who could help us.'

So they carefully hid the chair under a bramble-bush, and piled bracken over it too. Then they found a little path and went down it, wondering where it led to.

It led to a small and pretty cottage. The name was on the gate ... Dimple Cottage. Mollie liked the sound of it.

She thought they would be quite safe in going there.

They knocked. To their enormous surprise the door was opened by a brown mouse! She wore a check apron and cap, and large slippers on her feet. The children stared. They could never get used to this sort of thing, although they had seen many strange sights by now.

'Good afternoon,' said Peter, and then didn't know what else to say.

'Do you want to see my mistress?' asked the mouse.

'Well, yes, perhaps it would be a good idea,' said Peter. So the mouse asked them in and showed them into a tiny drawing-room.

'What are we going to *say*?' whispered Peter – but before Mollie had time to answer, someone came into the room.

It was a small elf, with neat silvery wings, silvery golden hair, and a big dimple in her cheek when she smiled. Mollie and Peter liked her at once.

'Good afternoon,' she said. 'What can I do for you?'

Both talking at once, the two children told her their troubles – how they had quarrelled with Binky – and he had gone home – and been caught by the yellow bird belonging to the enchanter Clip-clap – and how their wishing-chair had brought them to the strange tower.

'But we don't know how to get into it and we are afraid of being caught by Clip-clap too,' said Peter. 'I don't know if you can help us?'

'I don't think I can,' said the elf, whose name was Dimple. 'No one knows a spell powerful enough to get into the enchanter's tower. I've lived here for three hundred years and no one has ever got into that tower except the enchanter and his servants and friends. I wouldn't try if I were you.'

'We *must*,' said Mollie. 'You see, Binky is our own friend – and we must help him.'

'Yes – we have to help our friends,' said the elf. 'Wait a minute – I wonder if my mouse knows anything that might help us. Harriet! Harriet!'

The little servant mouse came running in. 'Yes, Madam,' she said.

'Harriet, these children want to get into the enchanter's tower,' said Dimple. 'Do you know of any way in?'

'Well yes, Madam, I do,' said Harriet.

'Oh, do you!' cried Mollie, in delight. 'Do, do tell us, Harriet!'

'My auntie lives down in the cellars of the tower,' said the little mouse. 'Sometimes, on my afternoon off, I go to see her.'

'And how do you get into the tower?' asked Dimple.

'Down the mouse-hole, of course,' said Harriet. 'There's one on the far side of the tower. I always scamper down there.'

'Oh,' said the children, in disappointment, looking at the small mouse. '*We* couldn't get down a mouse-hole. We are too big. You are a big mouse, but even so, the mouse-hole would not take us!'

Mollie was so disappointed that she cried into her handkerchief. Dimple patted her on the back.

'Don't do that,' she said. 'I can give you a spell to make you small. Then you can slip down the mouse-hole with

Harriet, and see if you can find Binky.'

'Oh thank you, thank you!' cried the children, in delight. 'That *is* kind of you!'

Dimple went to a shelf and took down a box. Out of it she shook two pills. They were queer because they were green one side and red the other!

'Here you are,' she said. 'Eat these and you will be small enough to go down the hole. They taste horrid, but never mind.'

The children each chewed up a pill. They certainly had a funny taste – but they were very magic indeed, and no sooner were they eaten than Mollie and Peter felt as though they were going down in a lift – for they suddenly grew very tiny indeed! They looked up at Dimple, and she seemed enormous to them!

'Harriet, take off your apron and cap and take these children to your auntie,' said Dimple. So Harriet carefully folded up her cap and apron and then went out with the children. She took them to the tower and showed them a small hole under the wall.

'Down here!' she said – and down they all went!

CHAPTER 22
THE STRANGE TOWER

The hole was dark and smelt a bit funny. Mollie clung tightly to Peter's hand. It was strange being so small.

Harriet the mouse went on in front, and they could see her little gleaming eyes as she turned round now and again. Once Peter trod on her tail and she gave an angry squeal.

'So sorry,' said Peter. 'I keep forgetting you have such a long tail, Harriet.'

At last they came to a place where the tunnel widened out into a room. It was very warm there. A large mouse pounced on Harriet and gave her a hug.

'Oh, Auntie, you're at home!' said Harriet. 'See, I've brought you two children. They wanted to get into the tower, so I thought they might as well use our mouse-tunnel. It's the only way in.'

'Good afternoon,' said Harriet's aunt. She seemed just an ordinary mouse except that she wore large spectacles. Her home was chiefly made of paper, it seemed. There were hundreds of little bits of it, neatly made into beds and tables.

'What are the children going to do?' said Harriet's aunt.

'We would like to know how to get into the cellars,' said Peter. 'You see, if you show us the way there we can get into the tower above and perhaps find the friend we are looking for.'

'Well, come this way then,' said the aunt. 'But look out for the cat, won't you? She sometimes waits about in the cellar and you don't want her to catch you.'

She took them down another narrow passage, and then the children found themselves walking out of a hole into a dark, damp cellar.

'Goodbye,' said the mouse. 'I'll put a little candle just inside this hole, so that you will know the way back, children. I hope you find your friend.'

Mollie took Peter's hand. The cellar was very dark. A chink of light came from somewhere to the right.

'The cellar steps must go up towards that chink of light,' said Peter. 'Come on. Walk carefully in case we bump into anything. And look out for the cat! We are very small, you know.'

They found the steps. They seemed very, very big to the children, now that they were so tiny, and Peter had to help Mollie up each one. At last they got to the top. They looked under the door that stood at the top of the steps. Beyond was a kitchen.

'Do you suppose the enchanter is back yet?' whispered Mollie.

'No,' said Peter. 'We should have heard that clip-clapping noise if he had come back. I think we are safe at the moment. But we must hide at once if we hear him coming. And look out for the cat, Mollie.'

'Can we squeeze under the door, do you think?' asked Mollie. But they couldn't. The crack was not big enough.

However, the door was not quite closed, and by pushing with all their might the two children managed to get it just enough open to squeeze through.

They looked round. They were in a very big kitchen – or it seemed big to them, because they were so tiny. They could not see Binky anywhere.

'Come on,' said Peter, giving Mollie his hand. 'We'll go into the next room.'

'Meow!' suddenly came a voice, and a large tabby cat with green eyes came out from behind a chair. Mollie felt quite shaky at the knees. She knew what a mouse must feel like when it saw a cat! What a giant of an animal it seemed!

'Don't show it you are frightened,' said Peter. 'It has smelt us, and we don't smell like mice. Stay here a moment, Mollie, and I'll go over to it and stroke what I can reach of it.'

'Oh, Peter, you *are* brave!' said Mollie. Peter walked boldly over to the cat and stroked her legs. She seemed very pleased and purred loudly. Peter beckoned to Mollie. She ran over and stroked the cat too. It was a friendly creature.

It went into the next room, purring to Mollie and Peter, who followed her. This room was very small and was lighted by a candle. No daylight came into the tower, for there were no windows.

No one was in this little room either. A dish stood on the floor with some milk in it, and a large round basket with a fat cushion in it stood nearby.

'This must be the cat's room,' said Mollie. 'There is no furniture in it. I do wonder where Binky is.'

There were some stairs going upwards from the cat's little room. The children climbed them with great difficulty for they were very small, and the stairs seemed very big.

Before they got to the top they heard the sound of crying. It was Binky! He must indeed be very unhappy if he were crying! He hardly ever cried.

How Mollie and Peter tried to climb those stairs quickly! At last they reached the top and found themselves before a big open door. They ran in. Binky was lying on a small bed, crying as if his heart would break!

'Binky! Binky! Don't cry! We are here to rescue you!' shouted Peter, hoping that Binky would hear his voice, for it was a very small one now.

Binky did hear it. He sat up at once, with the tears still

running down his cheeks. He saw Mollie and Peter and stared at them in surprise.

'Binky!' cried Mollie, running over to him. 'We've come to save you. Cheer up! We got in through a mouse-hole after an elf had made us small. How can we save you?'

'Oh, you are good, good friends to come and look for me,' said Binky, drying his eyes. 'I hate being here. I hate this enchanter. He wants me to do bad spells, and I won't. I was afraid I would be here for hundreds of years and never see you again.'

'Tell us how we can get away,' said Peter.

'Well, the only way in seems to be the mouse-hole you came by,' said Binky. 'So I suppose the only way out is the mouse-hole too. But I'm too big to go that way.'

'Well, I'll go back to Dimple's cottage and ask her for a pill to make you small like us,' said Peter, at once. 'Then when I bring it back you can take it, and we'll all go down the hole, get Dimple to make us the right size again, find the wishing-chair, and go home. See?'

'It sounds easy enough,' said Binky. 'But I don't somehow think it will all go quite so nicely as that. Still, we can but try. Leave Mollie here with me, Peter, and you go down the mouse-hole again.'

'We'll see him safely to the cellar door,' said Mollie. So they all went down the stairs again, and were just going through the cat's little room when Binky turned pale.

'The enchanter's coming back!' he said. 'Oh, where can you hide?'

'Quick, quick, think of somewhere!' cried Mollie. There came a clip-clapping noise, like thunder, as she spoke.

The tower split in half and a door came. It opened, and in strode the enchanter, tall and thin, his plaited beard sweeping the ground.

But before he had seen the two children Peter had pulled Mollie over to the cat's basket. The big cat was lying there comfortably. The children scrambled in and lay down by the cat, hiding in her thick fur. Binky was left by himself.

'I smell children!' said the enchanter.

'How could children get into your tower, master?' said Binky with a look of surprise.

The enchanter sniffed and began to look all round the two rooms. The cat did not stir. Clip-clap stroked her as he passed, and she purred – but she stayed in her basket, and Mollie and Peter cuddled close into her fur, hoping she would not move at all.

The enchanter did not think of looking in the cat's basket. He soon gave up the hunt and ran up the stairs, calling to Binky to go with him.

'Go quickly now, Peter,' whispered Binky, before he followed Clip-clap. 'Mollie can stay with the cat. She is safe there.'

Quick as could be Peter slipped across the floor to the cellar door, squeezed through the small opening, and made his way down the steps. He saw the tiny candlelight burning at the entrance to the mouse-hole and ran across to it. In he went and made his way up to the mouse-room. Harriet the mouse was still there, talking to her auntie.

'Please, will you take me back to Dimple?' asked Peter. 'It is very important.'

Harriet gave him her paw and took him up the hole

out into the open air again. Then they hurried together to Dimple's cottage. Soon Peter had told Dimple all that had happened. She gave him another red-and-green pill, and warned him to be careful not to let Clip-clap see him.

Then off went Peter to the mouse-hole again. Ah! Binky would soon be safe!

CHAPTER 23
THE GREAT ESCAPE

Peter hurried from Dimple's cottage, holding the pill in his hand that was to make Binky as small as he was – then they could all escape down the mouse-hole!

He ran down the hole and made his way to the cellar. He climbed up the steps to the kitchen. He peeped under the door. There was no one in the kitchen.

He ran over the floor to the little room belonging to the cat. The big grey tabby was still in the basket, and Mollie was there too, hiding safely under the thick fur. Good!

'Binky is still upstairs with the enchanter,' she whispered. Just at that moment there came footsteps down the stairs, and the enchanter came in.

The cat jumped out of her basket and went to greet him, rubbing against Clip-clap's legs and purring loudly. Mollie and Peter crouched down in the basket and tried to hide under the cushion – but, alas! The enchanter saw them!

'Aha! I *thought* I sniffed children!' he said. He came over to the basket and looked down.

'How small you are!' he said. 'I did not know there were such small children to be found. What have you got in your hand, little boy?'

Oh dear! What Peter was holding so tightly was the

little green-and-red pill that was to make Binky small enough to go down the mouse-hole! Peter put his hand behind his back and glared at the tall enchanter.

But it was no use. He had to show Clip-clap what he had – and no sooner did the enchanter see the little green-and-red pill than he guessed what it was for!

'Oho!' he said. 'So you made yourselves small first, did you – and came in through a mouse-hole, I guess – thinking to make Binky small too, so that he might escape the same way! Well – I'll spoil all that! You shall grow big again – and you won't be able to creep down *any* mouse-holes! You can stay here and help Binky work for me!'

He tapped Mollie on the head and then Peter. They shot up to their own size again, and stared at Clip-clap in alarm and dismay. What a horrid ending to all their plans! They had thought themselves so clever too.

'Well,' said Clip-clap, looking at them. 'You won't escape in a hurry now, I promise you! No one knows the secret of making the door come in this tower but me! Binky! Binky! Come and see your fine friends now!'

Binky came running down the stairs and stopped in the greatest dismay when he saw Peter and Mollie, both their right size, standing in front of the enchanter.

'So you had all laid fine plans for escape, had you?' said Clip-clap. 'Well, now you can just settle down to working hard for me, and using those good brains of yours for my spells! Go and help Binky to polish my bedroom floor, and after that you can clean all the silver wands I use for my magic!'

The three went upstairs very sadly and in silence.

Binky handed each child a large yellow duster and all three went down on their hands and knees and began to polish the wooden floor.

'Don't say a word till we hear Clip-clap go out again,' whispered Binky. 'He has ears as sharp as a hare's.'

So nobody said a word until they heard the clip-clap crashing noise, and knew that the enchanter had gone out again. Then they stood up and looked at one another.

'What *are* we to do now?' groaned Peter.

'Listen!' said Binky quickly. 'I have a plan. Where's the wishing-chair?'

'Under a bramble bush outside the tower,' said Peter. 'But what's the good of that? We can't get out to it, and certainly the chair can't get in!'

'I'm not so sure of that!' said Binky. 'You know that mouse you told me about – Dimple's servant? Well, if you could speak to her, Peter, and tell her to go to Dimple and tell her what's happened, she might be able to make the wishing-chair small enough for Harriet to get it down the mouse-hole and into the cellar. *I* know a spell to make it the right size – and then, when Clip-clap does his disappearing act and goes out through the tower door, we'll fly out too! See?'

'Oh, Binky, Binky, you *are* clever!' cried Mollie, in delight. 'Peter, go down to the cellar and call Harriet. She may be somewhere about. If not, her auntie will surely be there!'

So Peter hurried down to the cellar and called Harriet.

She wasn't there, but her auntie came – the brown mouse with spectacles on. Peter told her all that had

happened, and begged her to go and tell Dimple, the elf. She hurried off at once, and Peter waited anxiously to see what would happen next.

But Clip-clap came back before anything else had happened. He set the three to work polishing his magic wands – but took the magic out of them first! He wasn't going to have Binky doing any magic with them, not he!

After tea Clip-clap went out again, and Peter hurried down to the cellar. To his great delight he found Harriet there – and just inside the mouse-hole she had their wishing-chair! It was as small as a doll's house chair.

'My auntie told me all that had happened,' whispered Harriet. 'I told Dimple, my mistress, and we found the wishing-chair. Dimple made it small enough for me to take down the mouse-hole. Here it is. Good luck!'

She pushed the tiny wishing-chair out of the hole.

Peter picked it up gladly and ran up the cellar steps with it. How glad Binky and Mollie were to see it!

'Now,' said Binky, 'I must make it big again.' He felt in his pockets and took out a duster coloured yellow and green. It had a queer-smelling polish in the middle in a great smear. Binky began to polish the chair as hard as he could.

As he polished it, it grew bigger – and bigger – and bigger! The children watched in amazement.

At last it was its usual size. 'Where shall we hide it?' asked Mollie.

'I say! Don't let's hide it anywhere!' said Peter suddenly. 'What about us all getting into it, and waiting till Clip-clap comes back? Then, as soon as he opens the door to come in, we'll yell to the chair to fly out – and off we'll go! The enchanter won't know what's happening till it's too late to stop us!'

'That's a splendid idea!' said Binky, at once. 'We'll do it. Come on – get in, you two – the enchanter may be in at any moment! We must be ready!'

'The good old wishing-chair still has its wings,' said Mollie, thankfully. 'Wouldn't it be awful if they went, and we couldn't fly away?'

'Don't say things like that in front of the chair,' said Peter. 'You know how silly it can be sometimes. Have you forgotten the time it landed us all into a chimney?'

'Sh!' said Binky. 'I can hear Clip-clap coming.'

Crash! The tower split in two, and a great door appeared in the slit. It opened – and in strode Clip-clap, calling Binky. 'Hi, Binky, Binky!'

'Home, wishing-chair, home!' yelled Binky. 'Hallo, Clip-clap – here I am!'

The chair rose up into the air, flew past the left ear of the astonished enchanter and shot out of the door before Clip-clap could shut it! They were safely out in the wood again!

'There's Dimple and Harriet below, waving like mad!' said Peter. 'Wave back, you two!'

They all waved to Dimple and Harriet and called goodbye. 'We'll send them a postcard when we get back,' said Binky. 'They were very good to help us.'

'Won't Clip-clap be angry to think we've escaped after all!' said Mollie.

'I say! Oughtn't you to go and tell your mother you are safe?' said Peter. 'She was very worried about you.'

'I'll go tonight when you are both in bed,' said Binky. 'I'll take you home safely first. My, what adventures we've had since this morning!'

'I'm not going to quarrel ever again,' said Mollie, as the chair flew in at the playroom door. She jumped off and flung her arms round Binky. 'It was horrid when you didn't come back. I didn't mean what I said. You will always be our friend, won't you, Binky?'

'Of course,' said Binky, grinning all over his cheeky pixie face. 'I would have come back the next day. I was just in a bad temper. We all were.'

'I'm sorry about it too,' said Peter. 'Anyway, we're all

together again, friends as much as before.'

'You'd better run in and show your mother you're all right,' said Binky. 'Mothers are such worriers, you know. You've not been in to tea, so yours will wonder if you're all right. Goodbye! Thanks so much for rescuing me.'

Peter and Mollie ran off happily.

Thank goodness everything was all right again! Good old wishing-chair – what *would* they do without it?

CHAPTER 24

BIG-EARS THE GOBLIN

One day, when Mollie and Peter were playing with Binky in the playroom, they heard footsteps running down the garden.

'Quick! Hide, Binky! There is someone coming!' cried Mollie. The pixie always hid when anyone was about. He ran to a cupboard and got inside. Peter shut the door just as Mother came into the playroom.

'Children!' she said. 'I've lost my ring! I must have dropped it in the garden somewhere. Please look for it, and see if you can find it.'

Peter and Mollie were upset. They knew that their mother was very fond of her best ring. It was a very pretty one, set with diamonds and rubies. They ran out into the garden and began to hunt – but no matter where they looked they could see no sign of any ring!

'Let's go and ask Binky to help,' said Mollie. So they ran back to the playroom. Binky was sitting reading. They told him how they had hunted for the ring.

'I'll soon find out if it's in the garden,' he said, shutting his book. 'Is your mother certain she dropped it there?'

'Quite certain,' said Peter. 'How are you going to find out where it is, Binky?'

'You'll see in a minute!' said the pixie, with a grin. He went to the door of the playroom and looked round. There was no one about. He whistled softly a strange little twittering tune. A freckled thrush flew down to his hand and stood on his outstretched fingers.

'Listen, Freckles,' said Binky. 'There is a ring lost in this garden. Get all the birds together and tell them to hunt for it.'

Freckles gave a chirrup and flew off. In a few minutes all the birds in the garden were gathered together in a thick lilac bush. Mollie and Peter could hear the thrush singing away, just as if he were telling a story in a song. They knew he must be telling the birds what to do.

In a few seconds every sparrow, starling, thrush, blackbird, robin and finch was hopping about the ground, under bushes and in the beds, under the hedges and over the grass. They pecked here and there, they turned over every leaf, and they hunted for that ring as neither Mollie nor Peter could possibly have hunted.

At last Freckles the thrush came back. He flew down on to Binky's shoulder and chirruped a long and pretty song into his ear. Then he flew off.

'What does he say?' asked Mollie.

'He says that your mother's ring is nowhere here at all,' said Binky. 'She can't have dropped it in the garden.'

'But she knows she *did*,' said Mollie.

'Well, someone must have found it already, then,' said Binky. 'I wonder if any goblin was about last night! They are not honest if they find any beautiful jewel. Wait! I'll find out!'

147

He went to the lawn near the playroom. It was well hidden from the house, so he could not be seen. He drew a ring on the grass in blue chalk.

'Keep away from this ring,' he said to the watching children. 'When I say the goblin spell, you will see blue flames and smoke come up from the ring if goblins have been this way during the last few hours. Don't go too near. If nothing happens we shall know that no goblins have been this way.'

Mollie and Peter watched whilst Binky danced slowly round the ring, chanting a string of curious, magic-sounding words.

'Look! Look! Smoke is coming – and blue flames!' shrieked Mollie excitedly. 'Oh, Binky, don't go too near!'

Sure enough, as they watched, the ring began to smoke as if it were on fire, and small blue flames flickered all around. Binky stopped singing. He threw a pinch of dust over the ring. Smoke, flames and chalk ring vanished as if they had never been there!

'Yes,' said Binky, 'a goblin has been here all right! When a blue chalk ring flames like that it's a sure sign of goblins. I wonder which one it was. I'll just go and ask the fairies at the bottom of the garden – they'll know.'

He ran off. The children didn't follow, for they knew that Binky didn't like them to see the fairies, who were very shy. He came back, running fast, his face red with excitement.

'Yes – the fairies saw Big-Ears the goblin pass by here last night – so he must have found the ring and taken it. They said that he seemed very pleased about something.'

'Oh dear! How can we get it back for Mother?' asked Mollie in despair.

'We'll get it back all right. Don't worry,' said Binky. 'As soon as the wishing-chair grows its wings again we'll go off to old Big-Ears. He'll soon give it back. He's an old coward.'

'Good!' said the children in delight. 'Oh, won't it be fun to have an adventure again! Where does Big-Ears live?'

'Not very far away,' said Binky. 'In Goblin Town. Listen – there's your dinner-bell. You go in to dinner and I'll see if I can get the wishing-chair to grow its wings again. Sometimes a little singing helps it.'

The children ran indoors, bubbling with excitement. What fun if the chair grew its wings that afternoon.

After dinner they ran back to their playroom. Binky met them at the door with a grin.

'The chair's grown its wings!' he said. 'It is in a great hurry to get away, so come on!'

Peter and Mollie ran into the playroom. The wishing-chair certainly seemed in a great hurry to go. Its wings were flapping merrily, and it was giving little hops about the floor.

'It thinks it's a bird or something!' said Binky, grinning. 'It will twitter soon!'

The children sat down on the seat. Binky climbed on to the back. 'To Goblin Town!' he cried.

The chair rose into the air and flew out of the door with such a rush that the children were nearly thrown out of their seats.

'Steady, Chair, steady!' said Binky. 'There's not such a

dreadful hurry, you know.'

The chair flew so high in the air that the children were above the clouds, and could see nothing below them but the rolling white mist, like a great dazzling snowfield.

'Where are we now?' asked Mollie, peering down. 'Are we getting near Goblin Town?'

'We must be,' said Binky. 'But we shan't know till the chair dives down through the clouds again. Ah! Here we go!'

Down went the chair through the cold white clouds. The children looked to see if Goblin Town was below.

'Look at those funny, crooked little houses!' cried Mollie in delight. 'And look at the goblins! Oh, it's a market, or something!'

The chair flew down to a busy marketplace. The goblins crowded round it in surprise.

'Good afternoon,' said Binky, getting down from the back of the chair. 'Can you tell me where Big-Ears lives?'

'He lives in the yellow cottage at the foot of the hill,' said a little green goblin, pointing. The children carried the chair down the hill, for it had stopped flapping its wings and seemed tired. They came to the yellow cottage, and Binky knocked loudly.

The door opened. There stood a goblin with yellow eyes and great big pointed ears that stuck above the top of his head.

'Good morning, Big-Ears,' said Binky. 'We have come for that ring you picked up in our garden the other night.'

'W-w-w-what r-r-r-ring?' stammered the goblin, going pale with fright. 'I d-d-d-didn't see any ring.'

'Oh yes, you did,' said Binky firmly. 'And if you don't give it back AT ONCE I'll turn you into a wriggling worm.'

'No, no, no!' cried Big-Ears, falling to his knees. 'Don't do that. Yes – I did take the ring – but I have given it to the Snoogle, who lives in that castle over there.'

'Off to the Snoogle then!' shouted Binky, and he jumped into the wishing-chair. The children followed – and up went the chair into the air. They were off to the Snoogle – whatever he might be!

CHAPTER 25

THE SNOOGLE

The wishing-chair was off to find the Snoogle!

'If the Snoogle has your mother's ring, we shall have to find some way of getting it back,' said Binky. 'I wonder who or what he is. I've never heard of him before.'

The chair flew on. Soon, in the distance, the three could see an enormous castle set on a hilltop. At the bottom, all round the foot, was a great moat full of water. A drawbridge stretched across the moat – but, even as the children looked at it, it was drawn up into the gateway on the castle side of the moat.

'There's no way of getting in the Snoogle's castle except by flying, that's plain,' said Binky. 'Fly on to the roof, wishing-chair.'

The wishing-chair flew to the roof of the castle. It was turreted, and the chair flew over the turrets and down on to a flat part behind.

Sitting on the roof basking in the sunshine was the Snoogle.

The children stared at him in astonishment. He was the funniest-looking creature they had ever seen. He had the body of a dragon, the tail of a cat always twirling and twisting, and the head of a yellow duck!

He was sitting in a deckchair fast asleep. The wishing-chair flew down beside his chair, and the children stared at the Snoogle. They did not get out of the chair, because, really, they hardly liked the look of the Snoogle. But Binky jumped down and went to have a good stare at him.

'Snore-r-r-r-r-r!' went the sleeping Snoogle. 'Snore-r-r-r-r-r!'

'Hie! Wake up, Snoogle!' shouted Binky, and he gave the Snoogle a poke in the chest. The Snoogle woke up in a fright and quacked loudly.

'Quack, quack, quack, quack, quack!' He leapt to his two pairs of dragon feet and glared at Binky.

'I've come to fetch the ring that Big-Ears the goblin gave you,' said Binky boldly. 'Will you get it, please?'

'You'd better get it yourself,' said the Snoogle sulkily.

'Where is it, then?' asked Binky.

'Go down the stairs there, and walk down two hundred steps,' said Snoogle. 'You will come to a bolted door. Unbolt it and walk in. You will see my bedroom there. In a big box on the mantelpiece you will find the ring. It was given to me by Big-Ears, and I think you should give me something in return for it.'

'You shall have nothing!' cried Binky. 'You knew quite well that Big-Ears should not have taken that ring from our garden. I believe you were just keeping it for him till people had forgotten it and had given up hunting for it. You are just as dishonest as Big-Ears!'

The Snoogle waved its cat-like tail to and fro in anger. It gave a few loud quacks, but Binky only laughed. He didn't seem a bit afraid of the Snoogle.

'I'll go down and get the ring,' he said to the others. 'Stay here.'

He ran down the steps – but no sooner had he disappeared down them than the Snoogle also went down – following softly behind Binky.

'Oh! He's gone to catch Binky!' cried Mollie. 'Shout, Peter; shout, and warn him!'

So Peter shouted with all his might – but Binky was too far down the steps to hear. The Snoogle waited for him to unbolt the bedroom door – and then, when Binky was safely inside looking for the box on the mantelpiece, he slammed the door and bolted it.

'Quack!' he cried, with a deep chuckle. 'Now you are caught, you cheeky little pixie.'

Mollie and Peter were running down the steps, shouting

to Binky. They suddenly heard the sound of the bedroom
door being slammed, and the bolts driven home.

'Stop, Mollie,' said Peter, clutching hold of her arm.
'Binky is caught. It's no use us running straight into the
Snoogle as he comes back. Slip into this room here, and
perhaps he will go past us up to the roof again.'

They slipped into a nearby room. They hid behind the
door – and as he passed, the Snoogle popped his head into
the room and looked round it – but he did not see the two
children squeezed tightly behind the door.

'Quack!' he said loudly, and went on up the steps.

Mollie and Peter slipped out of the room as soon as it
was safe and ran to where Binky was hammering on the
inside of the bolted door in a furious rage. 'Let me out, let
me out!' he was shouting.

'Binky, Binky, hush!' said Peter. 'We're just going to
unbolt the door.'

The bolts were big and heavy. It took both Mollie and
Peter to pull them back. They opened the door – and there
was Binky, looking as angry as could be.

'To think I should have been trapped so easily!' said
Binky, in a fury. 'Anyway – I've got the ring! Look!'

He showed them a ring – and sure enough it was the
very one their mother had lost! Mollie and Peter were
so pleased.

'Now I'll just go and tell that Snoogle what I think of
him!' said Binky fiercely. 'I'm not afraid of any Snoogle –
silly, duck-headed creature!'

'Oh, Binky, do be careful,' said Mollie, half afraid.
'We've got the ring. Can't we just go quietly up to the roof,

get into our chair, and go away? I'd much rather do that.'

'We'll get into the chair and fly away all right,' said Binky. 'But I'm just going to tell the Snoogle a few things first.'

The children had never seen the little pixie look so angry. He marched up the steps and out on the roof. Mollie and Peter followed.

The Snoogle was looking all round for the two children, quacking angrily. He was surprised to see them coming up the steps – and even more surprised to see Binky, whom he thought was safely bolted in the room below.

'Now, look here, Snoogle,' said Binky boldly, walking right up to the surprised creature, 'how *dare* you try to capture me like that? I am a pixie – yes, and a powerful one too. I can do spells that would frighten you. Shall I turn you into a black beetle – or a tadpole – or a wasp without a sting?'

To the children's surprise, the Snoogle looked very much frightened. He was such a big creature compared with Binky – it seemed strange that he should be so scared of him.

'I've a good mind to fly off in our chair to the Pixie King and complain of you,' said Binky. 'You will have your castle taken away from you then, for daring to interfere with a pixie.'

'No one can get me out of my castle,' said the Snoogle, in a quacking sort of voice. 'I have a big moat round – and a drawbridge that I can keep drawn up for months on end. Do your worst, stupid little pixie!'

'Very well, then, I will!' said Binky. 'But just to go on

with – take that, you silly Snoogle!'

Binky took hold of the Snoogle's waving tail and pulled it hard. Naughty Binky! There was no need to do a thing like that. It made the Snoogle very angry indeed ... but he did not dare to touch Binky or the children, for he really was afraid of Binky's magic.

But the Snoogle was not afraid of the wishing-chair. He ran to it and stood by it. 'You shall not fly off in your chair now!' he quacked loudly. 'Aha! That will punish you.'

'Oh yes, we will!' shouted Binky, and he ran to push the Snoogle away – but, oh dear, oh dear, whatever do you suppose the Snoogle did? With four hard pecks he pecked off the red wings of the poor wishing-chair! There they lay on the ground, four bunches of red feathers!

'Oh! You wicked creature!' shouted Mollie, in a rage. 'You have spoilt our lovely, lovely wishing-chair! Oh, how could you do a thing like that! Oh, Binky, why did you make the Snoogle angry? Look what he's done?'

Mollie burst into tears. She couldn't bear to see the wings of the wishing-chair on the ground, instead of flapping away merrily on its legs. Peter turned pale. He did not know how they would get home now.

Binky was full of horror. He had not thought that such a thing would happen – but it was done now!

'Well, I think you'll agree that you can't fly away now,' said the Snoogle, with a grin. 'Take your chair and go down into the kitchen. You can live there now. No one ever comes here – and you can't get out – so we shall be nice company for one another!'

Binky picked up the chair. The three of them walked down the steps very sorrowfully.

'We are in a pretty fix now!' said Peter gloomily. 'I don't know what we are going to do now that our wishing-chair can't fly!'

CHAPTER 26

THE SNOOGLE'S CASTLE

The children and Binky carried the wishing-chair down to the Snoogle's kitchen. This was a big bare stone place with a huge fire roaring in the grate.

Binky stood the chair down on the stone floor and sat in it, looking very gloomy.

'I know it was my fault that the wishing-chair's wings were pecked off,' he said to the others. 'Don't cry, Mollie. There must be some way of getting out of the Snoogle's castle.'

'I'm not crying because I'm afraid we can't escape,' said Mollie. 'I'm crying because of the poor wishing-chair. Is this the end of all our flying adventures? It is horrid to think we may never go any more!'

'Don't think about that,' said Binky. 'The first thing is – can we possibly get out of here? Where is the Snoogle, I wonder?'

'Here!' said the quacking voice of the duck-headed Snoogle, and he looked into the kitchen. 'If you want any tea, there are cakes in the larder – and you might make some tea and put some cakes on a plate for me too.'

'I suppose we might as well do what he says,' said Peter. He went to the larder and looked inside. He saw a tin there with CAKES printed on it. Inside there were some fine chocolate buns. The children put some on a plate for themselves and some on a plate for the Snoogle. Mollie put the kettle on the fire to boil. They all waited for the steam to come out – but nobody said a word. They were too unhappy.

When the kettle boiled Mollie made tea in two teapots. She took one teapot, cup and saucer, and plate of cakes to the Snoogle, who was sitting in the dining-room reading a newspaper. It was upside down, so Mollie didn't think it was much use to him. But she was too polite to say so. She couldn't help feeling, too, that it would be much better for all of them if they tried to be friendly with the Snoogle.

She put the tray down by the Snoogle and left him. He opened his great beak before she was out of the room and gobbled up one cake after another. Mollie thought he must be a very greedy creature.

She went back to the kitchen, and she and the others munched chocolate buns and drank hot tea, wondering gloomily what to do next.

'Perhaps we could swim across that moat,' said Mollie at last.

'We'll look and see, when we can creep away for a few minutes,' said Peter.

'Listen,' said Binky. 'What's that noise?'

'Snore-r-r-r-r-r! Snore-r-r-r-r-r!' went the Snoogle in the dining-room. The three looked at one another.

'What about poking all round to see if there's any way of escape now?' whispered Peter.

'Come on, then!' said Binky. They all got up. They went

to the kitchen door and opened it. It looked straight on to the moat. How wide and deep and cold it looked!

'Ooh!' said Mollie. 'I'd never be able to swim across that, I'm sure. Nor would you, Peter!'

'And look!' said Binky, pointing down into the water. 'There are giant frogs there – they would bite us, I expect!'

Sure enough, as Mollie and Peter peered down into the water they saw the blunt snouts of many giant frogs. 'Oooh!' said Mollie. 'I'm not going to jump in there!'

'I say!' said Peter. 'What about the drawbridge? Couldn't we let that down ourselves and escape that way?'

'Of course!' said Binky. 'Come on. We'll find it before the old Snoogle awakes.'

They went through the kitchen and into a big wide hall. They swung open the great front door. A path led down to a gateway that overlooked the moat. The door of the gateway was the drawbridge, drawn up over the entrance.

The three ran down to the gate. Binky looked carefully at the chains that held up the drawbridge.

'Look!' he said to the others. 'These chains are fastened by a padlock. The drawbridge cannot be let down unless the key is fitted into the padlock and the lock is turned. Then the drawbridge will be let down over the moat.'

'Where is the key to the padlock, I wonder,' said Mollie.

'I know,' said Peter. 'The Snoogle has it. I saw a big key hanging from him somewhere.'

'Can't we get it?' asked Mollie. 'He's asleep. Let's try.'

They tiptoed into the dining-room. The Snoogle was certainly very fast asleep.

'I guess we can get the key without waking him!' whispered Binky, in delight. 'Where is it?'

They looked all round the Snoogle for the key – but they couldn't see it. And then, at last, Peter saw it – or part of it. The Snoogle was sitting on it! They could just see the head of the key sticking out from underneath him.

'No good,' said Binky, shaking his head and tiptoeing out. 'We should certainly wake him if we tried to pull that key out, as he's sitting on it. I suppose that's why he sat on it, to stop us getting it!'

'Anyway, I expect the drawbridge would have made an awful noise rattling down on its chains,' said Peter gloomily. 'The Snoogle would have heard it and woken up and come after us.'

'What shall we do now?' said Mollie, in despair. 'We can't swim the moat. We can't unlock the drawbridge and let it down.'

'There's one thing we might try,' said Binky. 'I might try to whistle one of the birds down to a windowsill and tell it of our dreadful fix. It would fly back to pixie-land and perhaps the King would send to rescue us. You never know.'

'Yes – do that,' said Mollie, cheering up. The children and the pixie went up the stairs and into a bedroom. They leaned out of the open window. Below lay the silvery moat.

Binky began to whistle. It was a soft whistle, but a very piercing one. Mollie felt sure that if she had been a bird she would have come in answer to Binky's whistle.

Binky stopped his whistling. He looked anxiously into the sky and waited. No bird came. No bird was to be seen.

'I'll try again,' said Binky. He whistled once more. They waited, looking everywhere for the sign of a bird.

'There are no birds in this Snoogle country,' said the pixie, with a sigh. 'One would have come if it could.'

'Well,' said Mollie, looking worried, 'whatever can we do now? There doesn't seem to be any way of escape at all – nor any way of getting people to help us.'

'Let's go into each of the rooms, upstairs and downstairs, and see if there is anyone there,' said Binky. 'We might find a servant or someone – they might help us. You never know!'

So the children and the pixie went into each room, one by one. They were queer, untidy rooms. It looked as if the Snoogle lived in one for a bit and then, when it became too untidy, went into another one and lived there until the same thing happened!

There was no one at all in any of the rooms. Only the Snoogle lived in the castle, that was plain.

'Well, we've been in many fixes,' said the pixie gloomily, 'but this is about the tightest fix we've ever been in. How I hate the Snoogle for pecking the wings off our dear old wishing-chair!'

The children and Binky went down into the kitchen again. The Snoogle was no longer snoring in the dining-room. He must be awake!

He was. He came into the kitchen, snapping his duck-beak and waving his cat's tail.

'Well,' he said, with a grin. 'Been all over the castle to find a way of escape? Aha! You won't find that in a hurry! Well, as you're here, you may as well wait on me. I'm tired of doing my own cooking and washing-up. You can do it for me.'

'We won't, then!' said Peter furiously. 'It is bad enough to have to be here, without waiting on a duck-headed creature like you!'

'Hush, Peter,' said Mollie suddenly. 'Hush! Very well, Snoogle, we will do as you say. Where would you like your supper? There is a cloth in the drawer, but it is dirty. Have you a clean one, so that I can begin to get your supper for you?'

'You are a sensible girl,' said the Snoogle, pleased. 'I have a clean cloth upstairs. I will get it.'

He went out of the room. Binky and Peter turned and stared at Mollie in amazement. What did she mean by giving in so meekly to the horrid Snoogle?

'Peter! Binky! Look!' said Mollie, and she pointed to the wishing-chair, where it stood in a corner of the kitchen. The others looked – and whatever do you suppose they saw? Guess?

The wishing-chair was growing new wings! Yes, really! Tiny red buds were forming on its legs. They grew fast. They burst into feathers. They were growing into new, strong wings!

'Goodness!' said Peter and Binky, amazed. 'Who would have thought of that! Good old wishing-chair!'

'Quick – here comes the Snoogle. Put the chair behind the table, where he can't see its wings growing,' said Mollie. So Binky pushed it behind the table just in time. The Snoogle pattered in, and held out a clean cloth to Mollie.

'Thank you,' said the little girl politely. 'And have you got some egg-cups, please? I will boil you some eggs for supper.'

The Snoogle trotted out to fetch some egg-cups. As soon as he was gone, Mollie, Peter, and Binky crowded into the wishing-chair.

'Home, as quickly as you can, wishing-chair!' shouted Binky. The chair flapped its new red wings and rose into the air. The Snoogle came running into the kitchen. He quacked with rage. He tried to get hold of the chair as it flew past him.

Binky kicked out at him and caught him on his big yellow beak. The Snoogle gave a squawk and sat down suddenly.

'Goodbye, goodbye, dear Snoogle!' yelled Binky, waving his hand. '*Do* call in and see us when you are passing, and we'll give you a clean cloth for tea and boil you some eggs!'

The chair flew home at a great rate. At last it came to the playroom and flew into it. It set itself down on the floor, and its wings gave one more flap and vanished.

'Ha! The old wishing-chair is tired!' said Binky. 'I don't wonder! I hope it will soon grow its wings again. We do have some adventures, don't we, children!'

'Where's Mother's ring, Binky?' asked Peter, suddenly remembering why they had gone adventuring – to get his mother's lost ring!

'Here you are,' said Binky, and he gave Peter the ring. 'Won't your mother be pleased! She won't guess what a lot of adventures we had getting back her ring for her!'

Peter and Mollie ran off happily. They called their mother and gave her her ring. 'You *had* dropped it in the garden, Mother,' said Peter.

'Thank you! You *are* kind children to find it for me!' said Mother. But she didn't guess that Big-Ears the goblin had stolen it – and that the Snoogle had had it too! No – that was the children's secret.